BUENOS AIRES
TRIAD

F.E. BEYER

Contents

1

THE SPOTTER

A phalanx of drivers waited at the front of the arrivals hall. Standing with the others, Lucas had a sign for a certain Jorge Martínez: a passenger who would never arrive. Lucas was there to make an important decision, not to drive somebody into town. He thought it would be agony to choose. Who in the sea of heads would have a valuable watch, cash, and other expensive items on them? Even taking the precaution of staying away from Rolexes, he still might choose someone with a fake watch. What then? Once people started coming out the gate, his doubts faded and he found himself enjoying the experience. A tall man, he had a clear view over the drivers in front of him. Because flights from the USA and Europe had landed at the same time, passengers flooded into the terminal. The earrings and minimalist gold watch of an elegant woman, likely French, drew his attention. So did the iPhone of an American in puke-green shorts; a character already filming his holiday. With many potential targets on display, this was people-watching with a purpose. For Lucas, it was like observing beautiful women entering a crowded bar – each of them left unengaged would cause a small feeling of loss, quickly forgotten when the next one came into view.

He didn't take long to make his choice: an old European couple. Lucas had to get right up next to the man to confirm he was wearing a very expensive Patek Philippe, but in the crowded terminal this wasn't hard. He could sense the tiredness of the old man, a level of fatigue unknown to someone Lucas's age. *What a watch! Why arrive in Argentina with such a target on your wrist?* Following the couple to the taxi counter, he sent a message to the Venezuelans waiting outside: "Man short and bald, woman with long grey hair, red blouse. His watch is most important." At the counter the old man yelled out, his face angry. This didn't surprise Lucas – he could guess what was going on.

Lucas didn't leave the terminal right away because he didn't want the Venezuelans to see his face. He told himself this was paranoia, they had no way of knowing who the spotter was. He also worried that the target would get lost in the crowd, but soon enough a reply came: "We've got them, following."

Thirty minutes later, Lucas took an Uber into town. Although already after midday when he opened the shop, it was unlikely he'd lost much business – maybe somebody wanting a new strap or battery. Apart from watches, he sold small soft toys: pumas, bunnies, condors, and deer. He'd got a good deal on them. With no toy stores nearby, sometimes a kid saw the animals in the window and dragged their mum or dad into the shop. He'd also branched out into cell phone cases, but respected his father's wish not to sell jewellery. "Watch shops and jewellers should be separate," his old man had said. Lucas never got to the bottom of why his father had this rule.

From his spot behind the counter, sunlight showed streak marks on the glass display cabinets – they needed wiping, vinegar might work, but could he be bothered? His father wasn't there to shout at him, to tell him to get on with things. Half a block away the brakes of a bus screeched, causing Lucas a nails-down-the-blackboard shiver. He looked outside to see if anyone who had got off the bus would walk by. Nobody did. The view of the cobbled street bathed in sunlight lifted his spirits for a moment – thinking of the hours before closing time brought him back down.

2

THE TARGET

Exiting the plane and walking down the steps to the tarmac, Diana felt a thrill at being outside, but then she saw the line stretching out of the terminal. She didn't understand what was going on at first. Was this the line for immigration? With his hat in the checked luggage, her husband, Dinos, had the sun blasting his baldpate as they waited in line for the next hour. The melasma recently removed from his scalp with acid meant he shouldn't be in the sun. Once inside the terminal, they waited some more. *Surely*, Diana thought, *they could hire more people to stamp passports.* Their turn came at last. The woman at the booth didn't ask any questions, just smiled and said, "*Buen día.*" Then the fingerprint scanner took ages to read Dinos's sweaty thumb, and Diana could see he was nearing his limit. Luckily for her, their bags were already doing rounds of the carousel. No hold-up there. Mind you, they'd had more than enough time to unload the plane.

The clerk at the taxi counter claimed one of the hundred-peso notes Dinos gave him was a twenty. This was pointless, as eighty pesos were worth about a dollar. The hundred-peso note was light purple and the twenty dark red. In a flustered state, you might fall for this trick from a time when a hundred pesos were worth something. The middle-aged clerk in a white shirt with stained armpits still pulled this for the satisfaction of putting one over. However, his resolve melted when Dinos started shouting about a swindle. A screaming tourist is never a good look, and so, without dropping his cunning grin, he gave Dinos the correct change.

"I'm from Athens, we are professionals at such scams, been practising them for millennia, before this country even existed," Dinos told the taxi driver on the way into the city. The man, with creased beige shirt and crumpled face, knew no English and didn't look like he would give a toss even if he did understand. Diana wasn't feeling great. She was the one who had wanted to come to Argentina, and if the trip continued in the vein it had started, Dinos would be proven right: such a long-distance journey wasn't worth it.

The markings on the highway were worn, almost gone in places, but there were no potholes, and apart from the toll gates traffic flowed nicely. They passed parks with European pines and eucalyptus. By the side of the road, on grass several shades lighter than in Greece, men with big guts stood next to their vehicles. They smoked or gestured like Italians – especially if they were on the phone. Diana didn't know they were waiting until the last minute to do their pick-ups to avoid the exorbitant airport parking fees.

The Greeks got out of the cab onto a clean street with wide footpaths. Their hotel looked Parisian and the street featured several Beaux-Arts palaces. The architecture reflected a long-gone age of aristocratic prosperity. Perhaps it would be an idea to knock these buildings down to dismiss thoughts of such living. People wanted to believe the current government had cast them out of heaven. In reality, the last twenty governments were to blame. A red Peugeot and a motorbike with two people on it pulled up behind the taxi. The old couple was unloading their luggage slowly, easy pickings, but a police officer was standing on the corner, not five metres away.

Both hotel receptionists were busy with an ancient Englishman disputing his bill: "This isn't the price they gave me on Agoda!" Diana felt impatience rise within, then calmed herself by counting the number of lines on the back of the Englishman's neck. It worked. She closed her eyes and attempted a standing nap. This respite was short-lived. She heard Dinos yelp in pain. Someone had twisted his wrist – a young man, dressed in a River Plate football hoodie and jeans. Diana got a glimpse of his inflamed eyes that were too close together. A chaotic tug of war began. On seeing a pistol in the assailant's free hand, Diana screamed. Dinos had spotted it too, but out of fear, out of shock, he kept struggling. The man stuffed the pistol into his belt...and now both hands clawed at Dinos's watch. Her husband put up a fight; he'd been an under sixty-kilogram wrestler in his day. At some point, the pistol fell to the ground. The man let go of Dinos's wrist and picked it up in wonder. Had he forgotten this advantage much greater than his youth? He gave Dinos a crack on the head with the butt. Now his fish was stunned – he unclipped the watch, ran outside, and jumped on the back of the motorbike. For some reason, Diana ran after him. She shouted out to the police officer, who only followed the speeding bike with her head. What could she do though? Diana saw the policewoman was without backup or a vehicle.

The British man had scampered upstairs – the reception was all theirs now. Dinos sat on the sofa next to Diana, who held a handkerchief to his head. She saw blood on the sofa, but not yet on her skirt. The receptionist who took charge of the aftermath did so with perfect confidence and without a hint of sympathy. "I'll call the police so that you can get a report for your insurance company. That criminal was a foreigner. These kinds of robberies are happening more often. You can thank President Maduro of Venezuela for the situation."

"I can't believe it, so callous, they didn't apologise for their slack security," Diana said in the taxi from the hospital back to the hotel. "I don't want to go back to that place."

Dinos, with his head patched and a hefty dose of tramadol inside, said, "They'll make us pay for the carpet and sofa – there was a lot of blood." Diana knew he was winding her up, but became frantic anyway and started yelling at the taxi driver to turn around. This was more of a reaction than Dinos had bargained for. He pleaded with her to calm down and apologised to the driver.

3

STOLEN WATCHES

Six months after his father died, Lucas started buying stolen watches. The old man had chased scum selling stolen stuff or fakes out of the shop with a wooden table leg. Worse still, with a few exceptions, Lucas was buying from foreigners: a Paraguayan, a Senegalese, and assorted others. "Foreigners?" his father would say. "Pouring over the borders...thieves from Bolivia, former Shining Path guerrillas from Peru, born slum-dwellers from Paraguay. Do you know the Shining Path Lucas? Communist extremists who bombed the hell out of Peru in the nineties, then turned to drug trafficking until the Peruvian government kicked them out. Over our unpatrolled border they came, and are now happy and safe cooking up crack in the *villa miseria* in Bajo Flores. You see, Argentina is the country for your criminal businessman. The politicians don't care about protecting our borders, the more uneducated and poor people we have, the easier it is to get votes in exchange for a few bottles of Quilmes beer.

Unlike the Italians and the *Gallegos*, even the Arabs, these newcomers from neighbouring countries don't work. Your great-great-grandfather, Lucas, came here from Genoa in 1908. He got off the boat and a sign saying, 'You are here to work', greeted him. The oligarch families put that up. They had divided the land between themselves into huge estates and thought Argentina was theirs forever more. We showed them. Your great-grandfather unloaded boats in La Boca, but he knew how to repair watches, and here we are." Lucas tried to stop this lecture that had gone through his brain a thousand times. The guilt his father had felt when the business went downhill contributed to his early death. The crash of 2001, then some terrible governments, and other factors contributed to his financial problems. Ultimately, though, his father blamed himself that they had to shut the shop downtown Buenos Aires and rent a much smaller place in this southern neighbourhood. What would he think of his son buying and selling hot watches? And that was nothing compared with what Lucas had got himself involved in now.

The shop bell sounded, a welcome distraction from his thoughts. A familiar coughing and wheezing had come in: Dad's friend Arquímedes, a man with fantastic posture for a seventy-year-old. While most men his age leaned forward, he tilted his head way back to look down his nose at you. He could do this even with those taller than he was, and with Lucas he gave away about fifteen centimetres. Lucas imagined the hours of stretches Arquímedes did to maintain his posture. Today this old man had a rotten expression made of pursed lips and angry diagonal brows. Had he queued for ages to get his pension money that morning? Lucas could see he wanted to take his frustrations out on somebody.

"My strap is broken!" Arquímedes threw a Lige watch on the counter. The top strap was shorn of the loop and buckle.

"How did it happen?" This question was barely out when Lucas wanted it back.

"What do you mean, how did it happen? It wore out. Made in China, wasn't it?"

"Yeah, but the watch is made in China too and you've had it for three years."

Looks like it's been cut with a knife or scissors, Lucas wanted to say but thought the better of it. "How about a quality Brazilian-made strap? I'll have to order it in."

"Brazilian made! More likely arrived in Ciudad del Este on a Chinese plane, smuggled into Brazil and then Argentina."

"No, this is made by a legit Brazilian company."

"Those animals couldn't make anything."

"Well, do you want it?"

Arquímedes' eyebrows lifted into high arches that shouted, *How dare you!* But he needed the strap. "Order me one." Then wearily, but with great satisfaction, he said, "I didn't get treated like this by your father."

"We used the same brands and suppliers when he was here."

"Perhaps you did, but it's the attitude that counts. How much will this Brazilian strap be then?"

"Eight hundred pesos."

Arquímedes extracted eight bills and slapped them on the counter. This was all a show, it wasn't necessary to pay now. He turned and, almost falling over backwards, walked out. It gave Lucas no satisfaction that paying the eight hundred had obviously emptied the man's wallet. He felt upset he couldn't have been nicer to Arquímedes – the likes of whom were his bread and butter. The ability to smile at difficult customers was important. Arquímedes was toxic, but he and his ilk propped up the carcass of a business that paid Lucas's rent.

The bell went again, and in came a well-lined forehead and expressionless eyes. The face would have suited a mechanic or a senior union rep. The man's tight blue shirt and black slacks didn't go with his mug, nor did his brown leather shoes, belt, and backpack. Flash clothes and that face meant a successful criminal, somewhat successful anyway. His name was Gustavo, and Lucas had agreed to work for him as the gang's spotter at the airport as a one-time gig. This was Gustavo's fifth time in the shop. On his first couple of visits, he brought in watches to ask their value. First a Seiko that usually sold for two hundred dollars. Then a Submariner that, despite being fake, was still worth a hundred. "You could get much more if you pass it off as real," Lucas had told him. "Just don't try to sell it to anybody who knows about watches." Gustavo got three hundred dollars for the Submariner.

On the third visit, he had a bottle of fernet as a gift: Fernet Branca, a brand said to be better than the rest, and hence twice the price. Not that he'd ever tell anyone, but Lucas preferred the lowly Fernet Vittone. Lucas found his visitor's friendly manner forced. He could imagine Gustavo, who was in his late thirties and only one metre seventy tall, as the silent thug backing the boss up. Smaller tough guys were always more dangerous because they had more to prove. As they drank the fernet, Gustavo had told Lucas about an 'opportunity.'

"They are easy, these tourists. They'll hand their valuables over without a fight and get it all back on insurance anyway. You choose the target, and the Venezuelans will do the rest."

"Where did you find these Venezuelans?"

"Oh, that was dead simple."

There was always a new group of immigrants more desperate and ruthless than the last. However, the growing numbers of Venezuelans in the country had made a largely positive impression. Whether you believed President Maduro was an evil dictator or a legitimate leader victimised by Yankee imperialism, it was undeniable that huge waves of Venezuelans were leaving their homeland to get away from his regime. Those who reached Argentina were often well-educated and well-qualified. They found work more easily than locals did, and this led to a debate about what was wrong with Argentine work culture. Lucas knew a guy, another old friend of his father, the owner of a restaurant in the upscale neighbourhood of Recoleta, who only hired Venezuelan waitresses. He was not shy about telling everyone why:

"They treat people well, and when there are no customers they find work to do, like cleaning or organising cutlery. Argentine waitresses have a bad attitude and provide snail-like service. Worse still, when you fire them they file a case against you. It's common for them to sue for wrongful dismissal and win."

Lucas himself preferred Venezuelan Uber drivers – they would ask what music he wanted and if the aircon was at the right level. Local drivers, by contrast, treated passengers as captive audiences to listen to their long lists of grievances against the world. Beyond the service industry, Venezuelan doctors were a godsend for rural areas in far-flung provinces that local doctors didn't want to go to.

On the other side, Venezuela was a country with an astronomical crime rate, and many hardened criminals were leaking out of there. Argentina was yet to have the problems of countries closer to Venezuela, like Peru, where the cops had recently raided a hotel and arrested one hundred Venezuelans suspected of being involved in organised crime. However, a number of Venezuelans were starting to get arrested in Argentina, damaging the hardworking reputation the community had.

On his fourth visit to the shop, Gustavo gave Lucas Dinos's Patek Philippe to sell. Lucas achieved this through a private Facebook group, and Gustavo let him keep twenty percent. *That was a beautiful watch!* Lucas loved the rippling Côtes de Genève decorations etched on the main metal movement plate and the warm glow of the metal face. But when Lucas saw the story in the paper about the beaten-up Greek tourist, he put two and two together and didn't want to have anything more to do with Gustavo and his gang. Lucas messaged him saying he could find another sharp-eyed watch expert. Gustavo texted back "OK," but now he was back for visit number five. He didn't have any watches or fernet, just another gig.

"I need your help again Lucas, I have another spotter coming down from Paraguay soon, but the team is ready to do a job this week. I'll give you twenty percent if we get a watch and ten percent of anything else. Here, take two hundred dollars now." He dropped two bills on the counter. "We need you, these Venezuelan kids are uneducated, they can't pick out a target with a great watch and luggage full of goodies, much like you couldn't be a gunman... Let me know by midnight tonight."

Gustavo wasn't a guy to piss off. He could report Lucas to the police for buying stolen watches, not that they would care. He could beat Lucas up or smash up the shop – again, no big deal. The Venezuelans who worked for him were more than capable of killing Lucas, but that would bring heat down on the gang.

Lucas closed the shop at eight and went upstairs to the apartment. He poured himself a large fernet and coke, and cooked gnocchi in a saucepan his father had bought during a brief flirtation with cooking immediately after Lucas's mother left. By midnight, Lucas was three fernets in. Sleep was impossible. He decided to go for a walk. It was hot outside, the air heavy. He planned to wander a bad neighbourhood a couple of kilometres north of the shop. This would take his mind off making a decision. When he got to the dodgy area, a downpour that had been threatening for days started. The rain sent the street life scrambling for cover: hookers with Victorian hoop-dress-shaped butts, trannies with cut-price Botox, pimps, thieves, drug fiends, and assorted ghouls. He had wanted to get a harmless thrill gawking at these odd bods; was there something wrong with that?

As the rain grew heavier, homeless people wrapped in blankets tried to pull themselves further into doorways.

He thought about kicking one of these wretches, really hurting somebody. *Why not?* Something he hadn't tried before. But would he feel better for doing it? How would he react to his own violent act? He walked on, mortified by his fantasies. A patrol car passed, the officers inside didn't bother with turning their heads to look at him. His greasy, wet hair fell into his eyes, which began to sting. He cursed himself for the situation he was in. By the time the rain stopped, his distress had dissipated, and he headed home. In the morning, he had a tachycardia-inducing hangover. After a breakfast of toast and eggs, he did it: he texted his decision to Gustavo.

4

HOLIDAY GONE WRONG

"I don't think I set the alarm, did you?" Robert asked.

"No dear...you always do it..."

"I'm not sure I did. Can we go back?"

Why is his mission in life to make us late? Jane took a couple of deep breaths. "I'm sure you've set it. Shina will be there at two to clean in any case, and I checked all the windows."

Robert's face was a sallow mask of anxiety for the rest of the drive. Jane ignored him and looked out the window as the midlands raced by – hedges, fields, Herefordshire cows... There was a long journey ahead of them. *If we weren't rich, I wouldn't have to bother with these overseas holidays*, Jane said to herself. Then she smiled knowing the horror such a thought revealed would cause her husband.

"What are you so happy about?"

"Nothing dear, looking forward to the trip... that's all." Having done some research, she had a plan for Argentina. *What is Robert going to do though? Eat steak and drink whisky most likely.*

Fifty-year-old Jane Steward, the press would report, lived in a stone mansion, a grade III historical building, in the village of Wickham, Northamptonshire, population three hundred. She worked as a development officer for the county. She and her husband, Robert Steward, lived an Aston Martin lifestyle made possible by the family business: the Stewards owned the Bandon supermarket chain. They liked Robert down at the local pub, 'The Schmoozing Cat.' He drank top-shelf whisky and was never shy of shouting a few ales for the townsfolk, most of whom, truth be told, weren't short of a bob either. Jane was slim and good-looking; Robert was pudgy, close to ugly, and sported a Boris Johnson haircut, but at least he was energetic for his age. Some thought them an unlikely couple, but mostly they were happy.

The British Airlines flight was from London Heathrow to Ezeiza in Buenos Aires via Amsterdam. They both managed to sleep during the flight. On arrival, their driver was waiting with a big sign. Jane had booked the hotel transfer, a white combi van with plenty of space. The driver had a stomach like an overstuffed haggis; he barely fit in behind the wheel. He was polite though, and sweating profusely insisted on loading up the couple's significant luggage. This was their first time in South America, and from the motorway, Jane thought the city looked like a rundown Madrid. The sky was clear and light blue, it was an illusion surely, but it seemed higher than in Europe. Along an avenue in the centre of the city, Buenos Aires started to look more like Paris. The neoclassical limestone Congress had scaffolding on its bronze dome – not a great sign for Jane, she reckoned it wouldn't be open for tours. She was right.

The continental vibe vanished as they drove down the hill to Puerto Madero. There, skyscrapers not out of place in a development zone on the outskirts of Shanghai stood out beyond the docks featuring Manchester red brick buildings. The van turned onto a street shaded by large trees and pulled up in front of their hotel – a revitalised industrial building – it looked impressive, as it should have: a double room for the night cost more than an Argentine teacher made in a month.

The bezel of Robert's Hublot watch was diamond-encrusted, but the crystal and band were tastefully plain. He now referred to this expensive piece of workmanship and calculated: "A twenty-six-hour journey door to door, not so bad."

The driver began unloading luggage. Jane and Robert got out to help. The driver stopped. Looking over Robert's shoulder, he had spotted something. He dropped a suitcase and ran to the hotel entrance. Starting slow, once in motion he covered the metres like an elephantine Usain Bolt. Jane was outraged – did he know how much that case cost? She had bought a very expensive set of luggage especially for this trip, not to mention the stuff inside! Then she saw Robert was in trouble: he was fighting on the ground with a black-haired man wearing a hoodie and jeans. For a moment she froze. Next, somebody grabbed her from behind. She turned and received a fist in the face. Her vision went blurry, but she aimed a kick at where she guessed the groin of her attacker was. She connected with a thigh and her wrist was released – through watering eyes, she made out a figure wearing a motorbike helmet. She ran for it...but had to look back. Robert was still wrestling on the ground. The man in the helmet threw one of their suitcases into a red car that had pulled up beside the van. Jane ran back and kicked the man in the hoodie, who got off Robert, then came at her and threw her to the ground. There was a gunshot and Robert started screaming. Jane was able to get up as the guy in the hoodie backed off her – and then she saw the man in the helmet had a pistol pointed at her. His visor was up now, such young eyes. He was saying something, "*Tranquila, tranquila.*"

"Bloody what?" Jane, with a lot of fight still in her, charged him.

Robert received emergency treatment at Hospital Clinicas before being transferred to the private Hospital Suiza, where he remained in a stable condition. The bullet had hit him in the thigh. Jane wasn't so lucky; she was shot through the chest and died in the ambulance. Her murder made the major English papers – this was a very bad look for Argentina.

The black and white video of the incident, taken from a security camera on the opposite side of the street to the hotel, appeared in the Argentine papers, but not the foreign ones. It was hardly graphic, the picture was grainy, and you could barely see the pistol. What was clear was the shooter's arm extending and the shock wave that went through Jane's body. Presumably, the *prefectura* handed the tape over to the federal police, who shouldn't have given it to the press.

The president addressed journalists on the matter. His small moustache twitched and he wheezed more than normal, signs he was serious. "The full weight of the law must come down on the perpetrators. We must find them and be severe." The president himself lived in Puerto Madero, he used to walk to work – he loved it, but since becoming president, his security detail wouldn't let him walk because of the danger. "The people of Argentina need to feel safe in the street. Tourists need to feel safe." The local press published a letter from the Hotel Association to the government, pleading with them to do something. This murder was one in a long line of violent incidents up to now ignored. Argentina couldn't afford a dip in foreign tourist numbers.

Police arrested the driver of the white combi, but released him after an hour of questioning. They had no leads about the attackers or the driver of the red Peugeot. Then, several days later, they found one of the armed robber's girlfriends. From her, the police got the name of the hoodie-wearing boyfriend and the shooter. The two men were planning to make an illegal crossing into Bolivia – not a bad plan, but they used their real Venezuelan passports to buy tickets at Retiro bus station in Buenos Aires. In the northern city of San Salvador de Jujuy, the gendarmerie dispatched officers to a house in the large *villa miseria* where the two young men were hiding. The press didn't report why they had paused before reaching the border. Once under arrest, the authorities took photos of both culprits on their knees with arms handcuffed behind their backs. To either side of them stood a tall, broad, and sombre gendarmerie officer wearing a camouflage uniform: a cruel image, but it sent a message. It recalled pictures of ISIS fighters with their captives, or terrorism suspects photographed with US soldiers before flying to Abu Gharib or Guantanamo. A dark place, most likely worse than either of those two famous institutions, awaited the young Venezuelans.

5

THE BOSS

A buzzing sound indicated the security door had opened. Gustavo entered and walked across the lobby. Several seconds after pushing the button, the elevator car clanked down the open shaft. He pulled back the old-style iron door and got in. On the fifth floor, a floppy-fringed Chinese youth ushered him through an entrance flanked by guardian lions. Outside the sun blazed, but inside the restaurant the blinds were closed and the lights on. Despite the pumping air conditioner, the smell of stale smoke was strong. Scrolls featuring either calligraphy or landscapes decorated the walls, and tired paper lanterns hung from the high ceiling. In this cavernous space that could have fit two hundred diners, Boss Ping sat alone at a large table. She was a middle-aged woman with unpleasant features on a face stretched smooth by severely tied-back hair. Compact rather than obese, it was unfair they called her Fat Ping behind her back. To her right, a man of about thirty in a white chef's smock stood nervously. Ping had a cup of coffee in front of her and in the middle of the table were two baskets of *medialunas* and a jug of orange juice.

"*Ta laile, laoban*," said the kid with the fringe without taking the cigarette from his mouth. The boss looked up and gave her guest the once-over. He wore a tucked-in mauve shirt that was tight over his strong shoulders, and blue dress pants. He had a calm expression, but a troubled history showed on his crisscrossed forehead.

"Sit, Gustavo, and tell Li how you like your coffee. Take a *medialuna*, we have *de manteca* here and *de grasa* there. Please get stuck in. Li can also get you some toast with *dulce de leche* or jam if you like?" Obviously not a native speaker of Spanish, Ping's voice had a scratchy quality, but her grammar was good and accent soft.

"I'll have a *café con leche* and two pieces of toast with jam," Gustavo told Li the chef, who hurried off to the kitchen. As her guest ate a *medialuna*, Ping started small-talking: "You know I've been here in Argentina so long I prefer your style of breakfast. China has the best food in the world, which you barbarians can't appreciate. And I say barbarians not as a racist term; in the USA there are people, like you descended from Italians, who love Chinese food. Argentina is full of people with conservative taste buds. But Chinese food is more suited to lunch and dinner than breakfast."

"I've never tried Chinese food, I wouldn't know."

Ping frowned. A decent conversation looked off the cards with this close-minded fellow. It didn't matter. *Business, always to business*, she reminded herself. "Where are the vehicles?"

"I had them scrapped."

"That was quick. What did you do with the plates and papers?"

"I've still got them – I'll destroy them?"

"Yes, do that. And what about these Venezuelans that were arrested, maybe they'll tell the police the duplicate plates and papers came from us?"

"I told them nothing, they were always going to be the fall guys if something went wrong."

Li came back with Gustavo's coffee and toast but he didn't get to enjoy them. "OK, Gustavo, stay in touch, I'll have something for you," Ping said, then she addressed the kid with a fringe in Chinese: "Get him out of here, Juan, I don't like thinking about how helping this guy ended up in a dead English woman. That's way too much heat. It's giving me indigestion."

Juan put his hand on Gustavo's shoulder and the Argentine got up from the breakfast table without protest. The look he gave Ping wasn't quite indifferent, but certainly unconcerned. Meeting with the triad boss appeared not to intimidate him, but, Ping figured, he was smart enough not to reject a job if she offered him one.

Three hours later, Ping returned to the same table for lunch. This time the stakes were higher for Li, and he keenly followed the trajectory of a tofu wrap to the boss's mouth. Ping's stretched face chewed around fifteen times before swallowing and after another fifteen seconds, she delivered her verdict: *"Haochi*...just as I told you to make it." Li let out a relieved sigh, his *yuxiang rousi* was a hit. He was now confirmed as Ping's chef. The boss continued with her praise: "I was afraid it was going to be too spicy, but no, this is like the version we have in Fujian." Most Chinese working for Ping were from Fujian, but Li was from Sichuan, a province famous for its scorching hot fare.

"My mother's tasted like this. She made it for me the day before I left for Argentina."

"I'm very happy you like it, Boss Ping. I can make you other Sichuan dishes at Fujian spice level."

Ping was disappointed Li wasn't at ease enough to ask: *How did you end up in Argentina, boss?* Being around the boss made people nervous and Ping had never learned how to make them relax. Her good humour came across as sinister. Li stood fingering his ribs. There was some flesh over them – reassuring, skinny chefs are bad news. His weight also protected him from becoming one of the boss's lovers: she liked them skinny.

There was nothing out of the ordinary in Ping's migration story. At the age of five, she figured out her parents would have loved a boy more. Attractive looks or academic brilliance might have softened the blow of being the wrong gender, but she had neither. With her as their one allotted offspring, her parents gave up on a comfortable retirement. For Ping, the options were a poor farmer husband or migrating to a nearby city to find a dead-end job. So when a cousin needed a supermarket cashier somewhere called Argentina, Ping jumped at the chance. After two years as a cashier, she found a way out: joining the triad. Someone prepared to shoot people didn't have their sex held against them. She didn't really like violence but preferred it to being bored. Many times, she had thought it extraordinary what she would do not to be bored, but she never had anybody to analyse this with. Especially now that she was at the top – the head of the triad didn't have friends.

"Can I go to the toilet?" Li asked, acting the meek schoolboy. The relief of the boss liking his dish had brought on a bowel movement.

"Yes you can, but use the toilet first on the left, not the one at the end of the hall. I don't let anybody use the same toilet as me. Do you know why?"

Li shut his eyes for a second as he re-clenched his buttocks, he wasn't going anywhere for the minute. "No boss."

"Night soil. It's my first childhood memory: the smell of shit coming through my bedroom window. We weren't too poor; I grew up after the Cultural Revolution. My father's carpentry work kept meat on the table. We also had a couple of fields of vegetables, fertilised by human shit. I never want to smell that again. Everywhere I go I must have my own toilet, and of course my shit doesn't stink." Ping stared at Li stonily for a long moment and then laughed. Li attempted his own laugh, which ended up more as a splutter.

"All right, you can go, well done."

Li dashed off, and Ping picked her chopsticks up again. This time she didn't bother with the tofu and stuffed the pork straight into her mouth. Her mind was already turning over an idea for deploying Gustavo. Much like Lucas's father, Ping was a patriot – or a nationalist. That is to say, she wanted to put her own people first: Chinese people, especially those from her home province of Fujian. That this was her attitude was up for dispute, because the Fujianese were exactly the people she exploited. However,

Ping would have countered that you had to make money somehow, and the exploitation would happen no matter what.

Li came back in and put a plate of fried green vegetables on the table.

"Sit down Li, have something to eat. When were you last in China?"

"Five years ago, boss."

"I guess they already had that pay from your cell phone in restaurants and ordering food online five years ago. I'd love to go back to China now, it sounds wonderful, so advanced. We need to change too, Li. I don't want our people having to pick up protection money anymore. It always leads to Chinese hurting Chinese. This Gustavo character seems steady and tough. I'll send him round the supermarkets. If it works out, we'll recruit more Argentines. What do you think?

"Yes boss, sounds fine."

Ping sighed; Li was a talented chef, but a hopeless sounding board.

"In my day Li, the extortion racket was brutal. The owner had three more days if he didn't have the money on the due date. After that, he'd be shot in the head. Because the assassins were Chinese, the family could usually find out who did the shooting. Then they'd try to take revenge. I've had a few guns held in shaking hands pointed at me. These days I tell my guys not to kill anyone, just shoot the place up a little, scare them, it works. It doesn't always go smoothly, we Chinese are nice hardworking people, but once we get violent we have trouble holding back. About six weeks ago in the south of the city, one of my guys shot a supermarket owner point-blank. He didn't have my go-ahead to do that and has now disappeared...to China perhaps? Since then we haven't collected in the south. It's easier pickings in the north, where the stores make more profit. But the Pixiu Triad has started visiting my areas in the south, not any stores still paid up with us of course ...nothing to start a war. There are thousands of Chinese supermarkets in the city, enough for two triad groups to prosper. But I hate losing ground. I'll try Gustavo in the south. I don't want him using Venezuelan kids though; look at how that ended up. They showed no restraint at all, shooting two tourists in the open...and for what?"

"It's hard to find good people these days, boss."

Ping put down her chopsticks and took a break from talking and shovelling food in her face. She looked at Li: the bovine eyes set in a moon face, the flabby neck and weak shoulders – the antithesis of a tough guy. He was right though, it was hard to find good people.

6

ESCAPE

His bus arrived at Rivadavia and Pueyrredon, the intersection holding the record for pedestrians killed in Buenos Aires. The main cause of this was people getting off a bus and trying to cross the road blind. Cautious, Lucas waited for the bus to move off and looked both ways before crossing. His tachycardia told him he wasn't quite ready to leave the city, so he sat in the plaza by the tomb of Belgrano. In front of the sarcophagus was an emaciated statue with dinosaur-size thighbones. It wasn't clear whether the figure represented the first president of the nation or not. To Lucas's right stood two women, the opposite of emaciated: Dominican hookers showing their wares, those being buttocks as wide as cars. They catcalled passers-by with *"Hola papi, ¿a dónde vas?"* or *"Papasito rico tienes un chupete para mí."* The hotdog Lucas had eaten for lunch rolled in his stomach. The vendor hadn't looked very clean and Lucas had smothered the sausage with mayonnaise, mustard, and tomato sauce, the chance of one of them being off was high. His heart refused to slow – nevertheless, it was time to act. He went over and bought a ticket from a Bolivian woman of under five feet with a hybrid accent. There was no need to show any ID to get an unregistered minibus up north. He chose the seat second from the front. The back was often the realm of big families with virus-ridden kids, and in the front row he'd feel pressure to make conversation with the driver. The only other passenger on board so far was a young man in a Boca Juniors tracksuit. There would be a long wait – the minibus had no timetable, it left when full.

The Venezuelan boys had been caught, but they'd never seen him at the airport. The police knew that some Argentinians had been involved in the logistics of the airport gang, but nothing in the press indicated they had any leads. For the president, the press, and the hotel association capturing the Venezuelans was probably enough. With them in custody, justice was going to be served. Well, seen to be served. Eventually, Lucas might be implicated though, and so it was better to get out. Or was he using the situation as an excuse to leave the watch shop and have an adventure? It was already dark when the minibus got going. The snoring of an old man and the crying of a sick baby carried on until midnight. Next to Lucas, a musty old woman kept him awake until about one-thirty by endlessly looking for something in the bottom of a plastic bag. Expecting it to be this way, he wasn't perturbed.

He woke at first light. Soon after they pulled up at a service station with dirty toilets, metallic coffee, and stale ham and cheese sandwiches. He slept again until they were passing through a villa on the outskirts of Santia-

go del Estero. Out the window, mangy dogs sniffed rubbish, and shirtless men rode ancient bicycles on unpaved
roads; both groups looked hungry. The city of Santiago
del Estero was an unremarkable collection of two and
three-storey buildings set out in the usual grid. At the
bus terminal, they had a ten-minute toilet break. The driver parked outside because only official passenger transport companies could take their vehicles inside. Lucas sat
down on a bench and lit a cigarette. He didn't smoke, but
on a whim had bought a pack before leaving Buenos Aires.
The terminal was quiet, nothing like the chaos of Retiro
Station in the capital.

Lucas observed a fat man selling hotdogs from a cart
parked on thirsty grass outside the terminal gate. Beside
him lay a young man, who, like the men on the bikes, was
shirtless. The youth got up and went over to beg from
some people entering the terminal. Then he took a cur-
sory look inside a couple of rubbish bins. Empty-handed,
he wandered back and poked the fat man, who laughed
good-naturedly. Lucas's heart sped up – this was the
world without the shelter of the shop and apartment. His
bus was about to leave, so he went over and handed his
pack of cigarettes to the guy without a shirt, who looked
up at him with wide-eyed awe.

The minibus ended its journey in a barrio far out from
the centre of San Salvador de Jujuy. The taxi driver didn't
talk – a change from the verbosity of the south. Lucas got
out at the main plaza. The shops showed signs of life as
siesta time was coming to an end. Restaurants, however,
would not open until eight. The only place serving food
was a Mexican joint with stale tacos and spiceless salsa.

They had beer though, and two litres left him bloated but with a reduced heart rate. He had plenty of money for a hotel, but where could he check in without showing ID? Getting to the border was another problem. *Contrabandistas* crossed over all the time and might help him, but where to find them?

The nicer neighbourhoods in the city were northwest of the centre, uphill in the hot sun. Once there, he spent some time in a café, enjoying the aircon and using the wi-fi. He had ditched his cell phone because it could be traced if they were looking for him. On a small tablet, he searched and found nothing new published on the airport gang. Through the window, he could see the Plaza Hipólito Yrigoyen, where kids watched by tired domestic servants, or indeed tired parents, played on swings and a slide. Old folk either walked laps or sat on benches in unending dialogues with a friend or themselves. In Buenos Aires all plazas had high iron fences, and they locked the gates at night. This plaza was unfenced, and that gave him an idea. He paid his bill, crossed the road, and checked the grass in the plaza for dog shit before sitting down. In his wallet he had fifteen hundred dollars. He took off his shoes and put five hundred inside each sock. It was a struggle to get his shoes back on. He lay down. Although it was nearly seven, the sun was still strong on his face. He found a shady spot, but the ground there was dusty, and he only had one clean shirt in his backpack. Tired as he was, he decided to walk around the neighbourhood until the sun went down.

Five hours of non-sequential sleep came at the expense of damp clothes and a cricked neck. By mid-morning, he was back in the centre of the city, at a counterfeit market selling clothes, sneakers, and DVDs. As he browsed fake football jerseys, out of the corner of his eye he spotted a very short man, almost a dwarf, carrying a large cardboard box. Lucas followed him through the maze of stalls until the man entered a shoe store, put the box down, and started to chat to the slim woman working there. Lucas went in and picked up a red Adidas sneaker. On inspection, the stitching was poor quality, and the label inside the tongue said *hecho en Brasil*. This was probably a lie. He could make out the dwarf and woman were talking about a TV show – their accents were Bolivian, which was all he wanted to find out. He lingered until the dwarf went out the backdoor marked 'staff only.' The woman, now unpacking the box, didn't notice Lucas exiting the same way. Outside was a grey combi with more boxes in the back – the dwarf grabbed a new load and headed inside again. In the driver's seat of the combi, a middle-aged man in a faded blue chequered shirt sat cleaning his nails with a metal file. It was worth a try.

"Are you going to Bolivia today?" The man, intent on getting the last piece of dirt out from under his thumbnail, didn't answer or even look at Lucas. The grooves on his cheeks looked like erosion-carved gorges. He had a worn, seen-it-all expression. However, when Lucas waved a hundred-dollar bill at him, the man slowly got out of the van, opened the passenger side door, and gestured for Lucas to get in. No words...that was it.

The highway out of town rose steadily at first, and then they climbed steeply through endless zigzags. At four thousand five hundred metres, Lucas started to get a headache. The driver, who coughed a lot and said little, handed him a mass of coca leaves. They tasted horrible, but he was too polite to spit them out the window. Along the roadside, guanacos, llama-like but brown and much more agile, munched on what grass there was. Finally, they began to descend. He could see huge mountains in the west marking the border with Chile. Below to the north lay an expansive salt flat and somewhere beyond that, still over the horizon, was Bolivia.

At the border town, they parked outside an adobe church. This was it: the northern *frontera*. A place of nightmares for his hardworking, prejudiced father, a reality for him. The driver told Lucas he'd be back in thirty minutes and left his number just in case. Lucas put the number in his tablet – he could borrow a phone if need be. The combi moved off, leaving a cloud of dust. Lucas wandered to the plaza, where Bolivians wearing woollen hats sold souvenirs: llamas carved out of wood, dolls, and blankets. The autumn sun was hot, but he guessed it got cold here at night. At a kiosk, he bought a litre of water, a sandwich, crackers, and sweets. He wanted to get rid of the last of his Argentine pesos – the exchange rate for them would be terrible over the border. The driver came back in a beaten-up green Toyota station wagon. There was a man in the passenger seat. Although less defined, he had the same facial grooves. *It's the younger brother.* Lucas didn't like this: it was two against one.

They didn't take any backroads to get over the border, nor did they stop at the immigration post on either side. There was no traffic hold-up, it was dead easy. The customs officers were all paid off, he guessed.

The quality of the road in Bolivia was good. The impressive, but monotonous lunar landscape belonged to a part of the world not yet under video surveillance. Maybe a satellite was looking down on them. But, Lucas reckoned, they wouldn't release footage to solve a crime in which the victim and perpetrators weren't important people. It would be easy to stop the car here, march him away from the road at gunpoint, shoot him, and dump his body in a ditch. Would they shoot him? No, crossing a border with contraband was one thing, but with a firearm another. They would whack him on the head with a rock as he took a piss. He'd fall and they'd crush his skull into the iron-rich red earth, a few shades lighter than blood. The four hundred dollars in his wallet wouldn't be a bad return. Probably these men didn't make that in a month, especially after subtracting their fuel costs. Would they check his shoes? No, the brothers wouldn't be so thorough. Eventually his body would be found, a week, a month later, and the police disappointed by a wallet with no cash. With the lack of ID and a flattened head, they could be forgiven for not doing much follow-up. The morgue worker would get the thousand dollars in his shoes, Lucas decided. He would be a deserving character smelling of formaldehyde, a skinny man in his thirties, who had never been on a date.

7

DODGY CHICKEN

To state the obvious, the streets of La Paz were different from those of Buenos Aires. If not clean and shiny, everything was at least new and interesting, and so walking around kept Lucas's mind from replaying what had happened in Puerto Madero. Late one night, after wandering for hours, he returned to the neighbourhood he was staying in. At that hour, the only option for his rumbling stomach was an eatery without even the usual salt and thin serviettes on the table. Posters of Lake Titicaca and the Uyuni Salt Flats covered the roughly plastered walls. Some were ripped and taped up, which wouldn't have been noticeable if they had used transparent tape. About eleven and tired, the girl who took his order wouldn't learn much at school the next day. If she went to school. The fried chicken quarter was tasty, not as dry as he'd become accustomed to. The rice was stodgy, but who needed carbs? The only other diner did. The mountains of chips and rice on his plate were rapidly disappearing.

Going by his girth and the way his hair stuck up vertically from the crown, Lucas pegged him as a truck driver. Lucas washed his meal down with a *Cerveza Cordillera* and paid the bill. On the dimly lit street, tangled webs of wires weaved by brain-damaged spiders hung on utility poles. Did you just put up your wire and tap into the grid? Every fourth building had the word *alojamiento* written above the door — most of their aluminium roller shutters were closed. Those remaining open revealed staircases leading up to small hotels in who knows what state of squalor. A few blocks on Lucas arrived at the place he was staying. A middling establishment not for fussy tourists, it was a cut above the joints frequented by truck drivers and labourers. The rooms were clean enough, and if you stayed for a week they gave a considerable discount.

He woke at five with a cramping abdomen, agony if he pressed lightly on his right side. After half an hour writhing around, the urge to evacuate his bowels came. The ten-room *hospedaje* had two bathrooms, both occupied despite the early hour. When one door finally opened, Lucas nearly knocked over the bald senior citizen who emerged clutching a newspaper. He sat in anticipation of relief, but not much came out either end. He was in for a horrible time — having absorbed the poison, it was going to make him hurt. The day was filled with trips from his room to the toilet. The following morning aches and pains came on strong before fading in the afternoon. On the third day, he gingerly made his way downstairs. In the shared kitchen, the face of old baldy darkened when Lucas walked in. The push had not been forgiven. After eating some plain rice, Lucas felt physically better.

The next task was to shake off the depression that had descended. Being out of danger and having nothing pressing to do, the adrenaline had drained out of him and brought on a low. A brothel might do the trick. However, he didn't know where to find one. A taxi driver could help with this. At first, he felt reluctant to ask, but finally the itch trumped shame. The evening of the fourth day, after drinking two beers, he approached a driver smoking next to his parked taxi. Middle-aged, in a yellow polo shirt with grease stains down the front, it was a surprise when this man was of no use. The next driver, younger, cleaner and thinner, was more helpful and drove Lucas to an apartment tower in a nice-ish neighbourhood. "Ring the bell for 8A," he said. Lucas did this, and a tired female voice came through the intercom, *"Hola?"*

"Hola," he replied. The taxi driver had not told him what to say next...

"¿Sí?" the voice enquired. He couldn't bring himself to say anything but was buzzed in anyway.

On the eighth floor, the owner of the weary voice opened the door. The perfume hit him first, then her badly dyed hair and death's head make-up job. Thankfully, this was the mama-san. She led him into a small living room. Even in the dim light, the chair she gestured towards looked grubby. He took a seat. She had three girls for him to look at. All had the distant glassy eyes of drug users. Lucas chose the most acceptable-looking of the three and followed her into a room. It was hot inside and smelled of an astringent cleaning product. When she took off her dress, he saw the waist-trainer. She was a lot less attractive with her clothes off, because as well as holding in her stomach, the waist-trainer had propped up her bust and made it enticing. Uncovered, her breasts looked like two sagging turkey snoods. The girl was from Paraguay. Her performance was efficient, vacant, tragic, and mechanical. But for the price what did one expect? Afterwards the mama-san offered him a beer. He had seen films with characters socialising in brothels. He did need some company but couldn't bring himself to stay.

Out on the street, he found his depression had lifted. The mild high lasted for half an hour. A cup of coffee halted the descent, but not for long. The only thing was to catch a taxi back and lie down. What was he going to do? Keep moving? He was living cheap in the *hospedaje*, but his room was closing in on him. The same nightmare for three nights now: lying in bed unable to move with the ceiling getting lower and lower. He would wake, panicking in the dark. Then he would reach up and feel only air...and so the nightmare's hold over him would be broken.

One day not too far off, his money would run out, and La Paz wasn't the place to make more. He'd paid rent for the shop and apartment before he left Buenos Aires, but it was due again soon... The press online hadn't published anything about the murder in Puerto Madero for some time...

8

EXTORTION

At the start of May, the temperature dropped fifteen degrees overnight. Lucas, having lost his coat in La Paz, hugged the warm empanadas to his chest as he walked down a street lined by jacaranda trees that rustled in the cold wind. It was a muted sound, as the trees didn't have many leaves left. Despite the cold, he was happy to be back. Seeing the architecture, plazas, and trees of Buenos Aires refreshed him. His dad would be rolling in his grave if he knew his son had hidden out in Bolivia. What did the old man say about Bolivians? Something about them being covered in dirt? He couldn't wait to take off his backpack, wolf down the empanadas, and go to sleep in his own bed. He unlocked the shop door. Inside, the half-full cabinets were caked with dust. It didn't matter. He bolted up the stairs to the apartment, which, by contrast, was cleaner than ever.

The intruder sat at the dining table. He wasn't eating or drinking. He didn't have a newspaper, phone, or book in front of him, and he didn't get up. With no teeth showing, Gustavo's mouth stretched out to the sides. *He's trying to smile,* Lucas thought. The attempt to look friendly failed, but maybe there was a reasonable explanation for Gustavo's presence?

"Your landlord came yesterday to collect the rent. He demanded to know who I was. But when I gave him some money he calmed down. I've sold a couple of your watches, but I had to use some of my cash too."

He'd paid the rent; that was great. Lucas realised, however, it must be an inconvenience for Gustavo that he was back – the shop and apartment could have been his.

"This place is insecure, Lucas. I got a window open easily and found your spare keys inside. You should have taken them with you."

Lucas put the empanadas on the table and checked the fridge. Apart from a half-full bottle of coke, there was nothing inside. He grabbed the bottle and poured himself a glass. That the coke was flat suited his still-sensitive stomach. Then he got out two plates for the empanadas. He didn't feel the need to say anything. Gustavo, his mouth full of empanada, did the talking.

"These are all meat. I wish you'd got some chicken. Anyway, the coast is clear; the police investigation into Puerto Madero is closed. Who told you to go hide out? I have a new job for us, less risk and more money."

Lucas noticed the most expensive watch from the shop on Gustavo's wrist: a Diesel Big Daddy worth five hundred dollars. He wasn't upset – that gold-plated monster had been a mistake to order in. It was never going to sell. Apart from the fact the apartment looked tidier than normal,

Gustavo taking over his life was a problem...but maybe the new job would be something to dispel the low that had travelled with him from Bolivia. When he was a boy his mother worried that he had the same mood disorder as she did. When he sat in his room crying, for what his father thought was no good reason, she would come upstairs and suggest going to the movies or an amusement park. She knew what boredom could do. When he was eleven his mother left for Miami, where she kicked her alcoholism, met a new man, and moved into a big house. She invited Lucas to join her when he was sixteen, but by that stage, he was too much under the influence of his father.

"Hey, are you listening?" Gustavo shouted. "I'm telling you about the job... I'm not a big fan of chinos, I remember the neighbourhood *almacenes* owned by Argentine families. They couldn't compete with the chinos and their mafia wholesalers. Those bastards, half their stuff is expired."

The chinos? Lucas knew there were other reasons they had been successful. The *almacenes* sold dry goods only, so you needed to go to the *carnicería* for your meat and *veduleria* for vegetables. The older generation didn't mind this – you got better quality stuff, but young people wanted a one-stop shop. The bigger supermarkets didn't offer an easy shopping experience either; they always had lines at the checkouts and never had change. In Argentina, a Chinese supermarket, *supermercado chino*, *súper chino*, *argenchino*, or just 'chino', was not an Asian products store. They were small Chinese-owned places stocked with goods Argentines buy, like cheese, wine, crackers, *dulce de leche*, long-life milk, and mate. The chinos sold meat and vegetables too, and owners realised that frequent trips to the bank for change were a necessity. The chinos were so damn convenient. Lucas didn't bother to point all this out to Gustavo. He wouldn't have wanted to hear it. It was the truth though, that in the capitalist race in their own country, the Argentines were losing ground to the Chinese and Venezuelans fast. They still had it over the Bolivians and Paraguayans, for how long though?

Gustavo looked around Lucas's living room as if he feared that someone could be listening. This was a sign he was about to get to the meat of the new job. "Lucas, you could use a haircut, but you're a presentable, well-spoken guy when you choose to be. Fat Ping wants someone like you on the job, someone intelligent and steady. We ask for twenty thousand for every new chino and ten thousand for those who have lapsed. Every time they pay, we take twenty percent. I reckon we can get two or three to cough up a month."

"Who the hell is Fat Ping?" Lucas put down a half-eaten empanada, his stomach cramping from tension. That or he still hadn't got over the Bolivian chicken.

"She's the boss of the Xiezhi Triad, and she wants us to collect her protection money." Lucas had suspected some major organisation was behind Gustavo. That it was the triads was fascinating and terrifying.

"Do you know what a xiezhi is?" Gustavo asked.

"I have no idea."

"A mythical creature from China. They have the head of a lion, body of a dog, and claws of a dragon. A symbol of honesty, the xiezhi has a horn on its head for butting liars."

"A symbol of honesty? Not a great mascot for a criminal gang."

"They have their code of honour."

Lucas was surprised Gustavo knew so much. Perhaps there was more to him than met the eye.

"So you are interested in Chinese culture?"

"No, hell no. Well, only as much as it helps me get business done. I can't stand them. Their food smells, and they never give you a straight story."

This answer quickly quashed the new idea of Gustavo that Lucas was toying with.

"And what happens if the supermarket owners don't pay?"

"You'll find out soon enough. This time no Venezuelans, we are going to handle the dirty work ourselves. Speaking of chinos, let's get some wine to celebrate our new venture."

"What kind of protection do the owners get for the money they pay?"

"None *pelotudo*, unless another gang tries to extort them. And by the way, if we see a pixiu on the wall of a new supermarket, we leave it alone."

"A pixiu?"

"I'll explain later, I need a drink, let's go."

Although Lucas was dead tired, he knew he wouldn't be able to sleep now. His stomach hurt, and maybe wine would numb the pain. In the chino three blocks from the shop, Lucas grabbed a couple of bottles of red wine off the shelf. He based his choices on price alone. Meanwhile, Gustavo was taking a careful look around the shop. They would need to be familiar with the layout of an average chino. This supermarket was too close to home to target, but in general, the chinos were similar. An Argentine manned the meat counter, a tranquil-looking Bolivian weighed the vegetables, and a Chinese lady with fast hands attended the till. A multicultural affair.

9

THE NOTICE

Fog hung in the streets of the southern neighbourhood of Parque Patricios. Lucas watched figures appear out of the white. The cold and limited visibility had them fixated on their destinations, a place of gainful employment for most. He felt protected – the fog shielded him from prying eyes. Nobody could tell what he was there to do. He couldn't hesitate forever. He had to cross the street and enter the supermarket. Running his fingers through his shorter but still greasy hair, he forced his legs into action. The Chinese man behind the counter picked his teeth with vigour. Despite being young and skinny, he looked tough. There was a phoenix on his right forearm, the work of a perspectively challenged tattooist. With no other customers in the store, Lucas knew it was time to act. He took a kilo of *Tacuarí* mate off the shelf to look like an ordinary customer on the security video. He felt ridiculous as he approached the counter. How could he make extortion sound legitimate? Nevertheless, he came out with the prepared spiel.

"I'm here representing the Argentine Association of Chinese Supermarkets. We have noted that your membership has expired. Argentina has a high crime rate. Armed robberies are common. We can protect you. Members receive a generous discount from our affiliated wholesalers. The fee for membership renewal is ten thousand dollars, paid in dollars, we don't accept pesos."

The skinny young man didn't look at him. He just scanned the barcode on the mate and said, "One hundred and twenty pesos." Lucas, his hands shaking, shelled out two hundred pesos. The cashier got four twenties back to him like lightning. "Maybe they'll ignore you, pretend they don't understand Spanish," Gustavo had said. "They won't believe you represent the triad. In that case, give them the notice." Lucas reached into his pocket for the A4 sheet. On it was a message written in Chinese. He unfolded the paper and handed it over to the cashier, who read it and frowned. Lucas noticed the nail on his right little finger was long and yellow, the sight of it made him nauseous. Still without looking at Lucas, the man got up and, paper in hand, walked towards the back of the shop yelling in Chinese. Lucas couldn't see the person he was yelling at and didn't wait around to find out their identity. Back in the foggy cold, his nerves calmed down. Gustavo was waiting a block away on a motorbike.

"Did you deliver the message?"

"Yep"

"How was it?"

"Horrible, the guy working there gave me the creeps. I don't want to deal with him again."

"Well, you'll have to."

***

About every five minutes, an attractive girl would pass the supermarket. Or was it the same person walking around the block many times? They were all slim with defined cheeks, an Italian nose, and long brown hair tied in a ponytail. They wore a black or grey coat, blue jeans, and boots. When the warmer weather came back, the coat would come off and a tight black singlet would show off olive shoulders. The lack of variation in the eye candy kept him from getting too distracted. He was monitoring the steady stream of people coming and going from the chino. Another time of day would have been better – the store was busy now. Finally, during a relative lull, Lucas got up the courage and walked in. He hung out in an aisle looking at pasta and rice until there was no line at the counter. He gave the cashier, a middle-aged Chinese woman, the notice without saying his spiel. Reading, her eyes widened, and she hissed like a deflating tyre. From the till she took out a stack of hundreds and held them out to Lucas. He pushed her hand away – he didn't want this chicken feed. He pointed at the number on the notice, now lying on the counter. "*No, no, no, veinte mil no, no tenemos*," she said, and then something else he couldn't catch because of her bad Spanish. There was no mistaking the fear and desperation though. Lucas walked out. He'd done his part and delivered the message.

He returned two weeks later. The same woman was behind the till. She didn't look up as he entered. Lucas grabbed a bottle of wine from the shelf, because no matter the result of his endeavours he would need a drink. At the counter, the woman reached automatically to take the wine and scan it. He held onto the bottle even though she gave it a tug. She raised her eyes. That she recognised him was obvious – her sunken eyes burned with hatred. "Wait," was all she said before walking with bowlegs down the soft drinks aisle and through a door out back. His mind raced. *Will she come back with her husband and he'll have a pistol? Is she calling the police?* She emerged again with a black plastic bag and gave it to him at the counter. The bag weighed about right. He walked out the door, telling himself not to run. The bottle of wine remained on the counter, but that didn't matter now.

After dropping the money at the apartment, Lucas and Gustavo went to a wine store and got two bottles of French Pinot Gris that cost five hundred pesos each. As they were choosing the wine, Gustavo slapped Lucas on the back several times. "Well done, our first payment, a piece of piss."

Lucas smiled, "I didn't think I could do it, but you were right, it was so easy."

Later that day they stood in front of a large map of Buenos Aires hanging on the wall above the dining table. The chino supermarkets in the southern neighbourhoods, which Ping had allotted them, were marked with coloured pins. Green and yellow pins indicated stores they had yet to visit: green for a new store, yellow for one that needed to renew its protection. Four blue pins marked supermarkets already visited and still with time to pay. Gustavo now replaced one blue pin with a black pin – black meant payment received. With the black pin in place, Gustavo said, "Cheers to us," and they clinked their glasses of French Pinot. After three weeks on the job, the twenty thousand from the middle-aged woman with the sunken eyes was their first payment. Four thousand dollars was theirs to keep. Success celebrated, Gustavo took a blue pin off the map and stuck a red in its place. Red meant payment overdue: action required. The skinny tough guy with the phoenix tattoo needed sorting out. They had to think of how to handle him.

"So this is how it goes down, Lucas: you stop the bike at the entrance, I'm on the back and I fire a few shots. The aim is to mess the place up, do some damage and make a loud noise."

Lucas took a gulp of wine. He had seen this coming. Gustavo wasn't very innovative. His own plan wasn't particularly imaginative, but done right it wouldn't send them straight to prison.

"From the entrance you won't be able to see where the person at the meat counter in the back is. The chance of hitting them is going to be high, Gustavo. The shelves might not stop the bullet. We don't want another person shot."

Gustavo looked like he was considering this, but then his forehead wrinkled up and he said, "We have to go hard, this is our first non-payer. If Ping thinks we're soft, we'll be replaced."

"I've got a better idea than firing a gun, and it'll make us look like we mean business. A Molotov cocktail. It will make more of a mess, be more spectacular, and is less likely to kill anyone. Also, we can do it at night while the place is shut."

After some more forehead-wrinkling thought, Gustavo replied, "They have iron bars over the door and windows, how are you going to get the Molotov inside? It needs to be during the day when the store is open, at night there is no chance of anybody being hurt. Why would that scare them?"

Lucas could see Gustavo was right. They had to throw the Molotov into an open supermarket.

The point of no return? Did he have to do this? Could he go back to selling watches, toys, and cell phone cases downstairs? No, with Gustavo in his life there was no option.

10

MOLOTOV COCKTAIL

Feeling light-headed from the smell of petrol, Lucas lit the soaked rag. A lump formed in his throat. If this didn't work, Gustavo would insist on a shoot-up – a recipe for disaster. It was an easy throw to make, the entrance to the supermarket was wide, and he could aim for the empty space away from the counter. However, this was no ordinary throw, but more like the penalty shot to win the World Cup. The pressure was intense. He could see the tattooed storeowner sitting behind the counter, serving a woman made shapeless by her coat. A couple more customers waited in line behind her. Being professionals, Lucas and Gustavo had practised throwing Molotovs. In the middle of the night, they had driven to a field of dirt way out in the province: a place where nobody would bother them. Their abilities in throwing the Molotovs were similar in terms of distance and accuracy, but Gustavo was far better at controlling the motorbike...and so didn't get the chance at glory.

Lucas would always remember with pride that he made the perfect throw. The explosion was blinding, and afterward a two-metre-square patch of flame continued to flicker on the floor. The cashier disappeared behind the counter and the customers put several aisles of food between themselves and the flames before starting to scream. The woman in the coat, the closest person to the explosion, had not moved. Her groceries were scattered on the ground, and she stared into space. In shock, she didn't appear to be injured. His work done, Lucas leapt back on the bike, pounded Gustavo on the shoulder, and they were off back to the apartment.

"I can't believe how well that Molotov worked. Great job," Gustavo said for the fourth time as he sat at the table sipping fernet.

Lucas, adrenaline still pumping, was frying a couple of steaks. "Yeah, it flew through the air perfectly like Maxi Rodriquez's goal against Mexico in 2006." Gustavo met this comment with blank eyes – he had no idea what Lucas was talking about. Not everyone needed to know about football, but it was something that could humanise the most unsavoury characters. Watching the game on a big screen changed hardened criminals from wanting to rob you to slapping you on the back and buying you a beer. The football hooligans had camaraderie, something to live for. *Hell*, Lucas thought, *even the crack addicts could blame their emptiness on the drug*. Gustavo, however, was a natural desert, a black hole who now slept in Lucas's old bedroom.

Two days later Lucas got some respite in the early afternoon when his uninvited house guest said, "Take a break this time, I'll go and pick up the money from the supermarket."

After Gustavo left, Lucas poured himself a large fernet and coke. He felt nervous but confident the tattooed su-permarket owner would pay. The Molotov had been an outstanding success. Nobody got hurt and a very small piece about the incident appeared in the papers. Gustavo had been unconcerned: "The police won't be interested in trying to find two men dressed in black, wearing helmets, and on a motorbike with plates registered to a vehicle in Córdoba. The supermarket workers won't cooperate with the police. There is nothing to worry about. You won't get anywhere if you panic at the slightest thing, Lucas. I've noticed when professionals break the law and do it boldly, mostly they don't get into trouble. Not unless they make a stupid mistake. Going half-arse is what gets you into trouble."

Thanks for the philosophical wisdom, Lucas thought. He had been the one to walk into the store and make the demand for money. If the guy with the phoenix tattoo did talk, Lucas would be the one in trouble... But now Gustavo was going to the supermarket to pick up the cash, which meant he wasn't worried about being on camera himself – this was reassuring.

He'd wreck his good mood if he kept drinking, so he put on his coat and went downstairs. Invisible from the balcony, a Senegalese man had set up his trestle table just outside the shop door. This character had tried to sell Lucas watches many times before, only occasionally did he have anything worth buying. On top of the purple tablecloth sat a selection of rings, bracelets, and necklaces. The Senegalese's face lit up when Lucas came out the shop door. *"Comment vas- tu mon ami?* You want to buy a watch?"

Lucas considered how to get away quickly. Should he tell the man to piss off? No, it was better to be polite. "Let's have a look at what you've got then."

The man unfolded all one hundred and ninety centimetres of himself from his wooden stool and unlocked a shallow drawer in the back of the table. He fished out two gold-coloured watches and handed them to Lucas – who barely looked at them before putting them on the table. "Chinese fakes...worth one hundred pesos, if that." Lucas wondered why the man kept the watches in the drawer, and not with the other shiny rubbish on the purple tablecloth. *Keep your marijuana, your cocaine in that drawer, but not crappy fake watches.*

"OK, I'll find you some better watches next time, don't be impatient with me." The man started packing up, muttering to himself in a mixture of French and Wolof interspersed with the odd Spanish swear word.

Lucas walked quickly to dispel his nervous energy. After some thirty minutes he reached the river. He sat down on a bench in a spot where the smell was unpleasant but not overpowering. He watched a jerky yellow catamaran use its long crane ending in a mesh plate to scoop up plastic, metal, and solid scum from the river's surface. It deposited the pollutants in a large circular receptacle. This curve in the river, a stone's throw from one of the biggest tourist draws in the city, was worth cleaning, but the catamarans didn't go further upstream to where faecal matter from the barrios and heavy metals from industry were plentiful.

The funds to clean up that crap had been embezzled, or so they said. If the river was ever cleaned, journalists would miss using it as a symbol of corruption in the city. A distorted tango drifted across from powerful speakers on the tourist drag two blocks away. He could imagine the muscly-shouldered, hard-faced female tango dancers putting their hands on embarrassed tourists' crotches for snapshots, while the slim-waisted male dancers didn't risk anything similar.

Done with the river, he crossed the street and waited two minutes for the twenty-five to pass. The bus was only half-full, and he sat down near the front. A baby girl stared at him over her mother's shoulder. Lucas looked away. Innocent eyes could be terrifying, but the child's cleft lip forced him to turn back. She was too young to be self-conscious of her defect, so his fixation on it did no damage. When the driver yelled out in anger at the next stop, he was happy for the distraction. Two boys of about sixteen had got on and not paid the fare. They had eyebrow rings, reggaeton haircuts, and stoned eyes. They were bad news. The driver didn't challenge their non-payment further, and the boys made their way to the back. As the bus sped up, one of them shouted, "Fuck you, don't text her." Then there was a groan and the sound of a body hitting the floor. Lucas turned around, one youth stood over the prone body of the other. The violence had begun before they'd had a chance to sit down. Repeatedly, the right foot found a vulnerable piece of the torso, no matter how tightly the victim rolled himself into a ball. The other passengers looked on the scene in a daze or averted their eyes altogether. Lucas got up, walked towards the boys, and pushed the aggressor in the chest – he was light and staggered back. He lashed out for a final time, but the kick failed to find its mark. The bus driver, watching in the rear-view mirror, slammed on the brakes and pulled over. Lucas aggressively gestured to the open back door and the violent boy complied. With him gone, the rest of humanity kicked into action and Lucas found himself outside a circle of concerned citizens crouching around the fallen figure. Embarrassed, he hopped off at the next stop. As he walked, he considered the unforeseen benefit of his recent criminal endeavours. Now he was a man who could act in any circumstance. There was no need to freeze or be passive. He felt proud of what he had done on the bus – no harm in that. It was strange though, out of the thousands of times he had taken a bus, this was the first time he'd encountered a violent incident...right after he'd thrown the Molotov.

Back home, feeling better for the exercise and experience, he settled again on the balcony, this time with a thermos of hot water and his mate gourd. It wasn't long until he heard a motorbike pull up and ran downstairs. Gustavo entered and threw a shopping bag on the counter. It hit the glass with a solid thump. He took his motorbike helmet off and his face wore an ugly grin. "We'll have to open the shop again Lucas, we are going to have a lot of money to launder. I need a fernet, strong. You were right, that Chinese guy was creepy! He didn't look at me, didn't say anything. But he coughed up."

Ten minutes later, sitting upstairs, Gustavo was already on his second fernet. Lucas had a question for him: "What are we going to do with the cash? Should we keep it in the apartment?"

"No, I'm going to take it to the safety box I have at Banco de la Nación. We can't have it lying around here. Home invaders can smell cash, Lucas. Did you see the news today? Terrible, an old guy charged with murder for shooting a burglar that broke into his house. What's this country coming to?"

11

DOLLARS

Lucas got off the bus in the microcentro. The foot-paths were chock-a-block with drawn-faced office workers. Tooting taxis and groaning buses dominated the narrow roads. Because of the tightly packed buildings, wind eddies formed on the streets and rubbish spiralled around until trampled down by the crowd. On Florida, the main pedestrian shopping street, vendors yelled out their catchphrases. The crazy tomato guy was the loudest: *"Tomatee loco, juguete para niños, tomaateee loco."* He was flogging what he claimed was a new craze in toys: tomatoes made of squishy gelatinous plastic. You threw them and they splatted and stuck to the ceiling or wall, then slowly peeled off without leaving a mark. Lucas had a snake made of similar stuff as a kid. Mixed in with the ven-dor noise was the monotonous call of the moneychangers: *"Cambio, cambio, cambio, dólares, euros, reales, cam-bio..."* Changing dollars to pesos was safe here if you knew what you were doing. Pesos to dollars was another matter, fake greenbacks abounded. REAL dollars were scarce. Those with employment contracts could exchange a certain amount of pesos to dollars each month, and the rest were screwed. Every day the newspapers published the unofficial dollar rate, '*el dólar blue,*' as well as the official rate. You got a much better deal out of the illegal money changes, a rate close to the *dólar blue*. Lucas was going to get for six hundred dollars what he'd get for seven hundred at one of the official money changes. A lot of this cash would go on some much-needed new shoes and clothes. Usually, he telephoned and met up with a man near the shop to exchange dollars to pesos. A guy who could be trusted, *una persona de confianza*. However, he'd done several exchanges with this character recently and he didn't want anybody thinking he had lots of dollars. This *persona de confianza* might not be so trustworthy and turn out to have some unsavoury associates. One never knew. Cash smelled – dollars much more strongly than pesos, and there were hounds ready to pick up the scent around every corner.

The reason why 'illegal' moneychangers could operate on the main street in town was simple: the government wanted dollars inside the country no matter what. Many people wouldn't part with their dollars for the official rate, knowing it was a fraud. The guys standing on the street yelling *"cambio"* were known as *arbolitos*, or little trees, in reference to the green dollars they had on them. First Lucas talked to a croaky Brazilian *arbolito* offering sixty-eight pesos to the dollar, not good enough. The second guy asked, "You changing more than a thousand? You get a better rate then." Lucas walked away: he didn't like being asked how much he had out on the street. The guy was Venezuelan or possibly Colombian and had a thing or two to learn about not scaring off customers. Lucas settled on a woman from Peru with a round face and non-aggressive manner. She gave a rate of seventy-two to one without Lucas having to haggle. He followed her to a small office in a shopping gallery. The diminutive guy behind the counter there was Peruvian too. Lucas had five hundreds and five twenties. The man told him, "I can only give you seventy to one for the twenties." It was OK. Lucas knew this was common practice with smaller notes.

After buying jeans at the Levi's store, two t-shirts and a jacket at Falabella, and sneakers at the Nike outlet, Lucas got an Uber back to the shop. By way of greeting the driver said: "You'll have to sit in the front, if the taxi drivers see I'm an Uber they'll assault us both." Bad luck, the driver was an Argentine ex-military guy in his fifties, who ranted almost without breathing. "Argentina is going to the dogs, ruined by immigration from neighbouring countries. No decent jobs anymore. I have to work for these criminals at Uber. The company doesn't pay taxes here...the money is going to the United States. I rang Uber to tell them I needed more rides paying cash. They didn't care. I can't go to Cabify because they don't work with cash and only pay out every fifteen days. I need cash in hand today. Some rides in Uber pay cash, but you need to stay away from tourist areas. Tourists have cash but always want to use credit cards, even though they have cash on them. You are paying cash, right?"

"Yes...yes. Don't worry. I get it, you want cash."

"I have an ex-wife, my mother...my daughter...I rent a garage for the car, which, by the way, is almost brand new and customers are wrecking it by slamming the doors and throwing their luggage around."

"How much do you make a day?"

"About four thousand pesos."

"That's not bad."

"You see if it's not bad if you have to pay petrol, the value of your vehicle is depreciating, and you have to buy clothes and other things."

Lucas then asked him how much he made a month. Assuming he worked twenty days a month that would be eighty thousand pesos, a decent wage.

"I couldn't tell you how much I make per month, I don't know."

"But how long have you been working for Uber?"

"One year, you can check my rating on the app. I've got 4.9."

Lucas couldn't help taking his phone out and checking, it was true – if this guy was a 4.9, what was a 3.9 like? A 2.9? The driver reminded Lucas of his dad. No, his dad was nicer. Hopefully he'd get a Venezuelan driver on his next Uber ride.

"Stop here, will you."

"Your destination is another four hundred metres away!"

"I know, but I've remembered something I need to buy at the supermarket."

The driver was still grumbling as Lucas got out of the car. In the chino, Lucas bought a bottle of Vittone for himself and a bottle of Branca for guests – with luck, someone other than Gustavo would visit him eventually. After struggling up the stairs with the bags of clothes and booze, he felt the tension ebb out of him on finding Gustavo not home. Holding off the fernet he sat down in front of the TV, mate in hand. Channel after channel of talking heads: men with eyeshadow, and women a mess of botox and silicon. The sports stations had second division games, and so Lacroze in his three-piece suit was the best choice. "They have robbed tourists coming from the airport again!" the Lego-headed presenter declared. Lucas felt an intense pressure behind his eyes. *Gustavo has started doing that again? They'll reopen the investigation into the shooting!* The reporter on the scene in San Isidro told it differently: "No Lacroze, it was not the gang which followed tourists in from the airport. This appears to be a lone wolf... A moto-robber pulled up alongside an Australian couple walking on a street here in San Isidro. He pointed a pistol and the couple handed over their backpacks, wallets, and phones. A passing motorist saw what was happening, did a U- turn, and chased after the criminal, crashing into the back of his motorbike, sending him flying...the latest example of vigilante justice in Buenos Aires."

Back in the studio, Lacroze turned to one of his expert panellists, a man with an enviable mop of white hair. "Feinn, this is interesting in the context of the Pilar case just gone through the courts that we featured on yesterday's show. Can you remind our viewers of the basic facts?"

"Certainly, last June the owner-operator of a wine store in Pilar was robbed at gunpoint. The robber left the shop with a paltry three thousand pesos and leapt on the back of his partner's motorbike. The storeowner rushed out, got in his VW, and gave chase. When he caught up, he rammed the bike into a traffic light post. The motorbike rider managed to get up and run off, but his passenger lay prone on the ground, badly injured. The storeowner recovered his three thousand pesos, took a wooden stick out of his car, and started beating the man, who later died in hospital... The courts have just begun trying such cases by jury. Formerly a tribunal of judges presided. The jury acquitted the store owner, finding he had acted in legitimate self-defence."

What? To Lucas this was murder or manslaughter at least. How on earth was it self-defence?

The camera went back to Lacroze, smiling from ear to ear. "Thank you, Feinn. Trial by jury is working; the public is much tougher than corrupt judges are. If you go out to rob, you forego your rights. Now an update on today's case is coming through my earpiece...the *delincuente* who robbed the Australian couple has three cracked ribs and a broken leg. The motorist who smashed into him hasn't been charged. Bravo."

Lacroze and his panel applauded. Outrageous behaviour, Lucas thought, but the kind of thing that kept the program's ratings high.

"The message is clear," Lacroze continued, "citizens have no problem with dealing out violent justice. They are sick of thieves and robbers. And now the judicial system is starting to back them up."

Lucas thought of the Venezuelans from the shooting, just as well for them they ended up in the hands of the police rather than those of enraged vigilantes. And he was not ignorant to what the story on Lacroze's show suggested his fate might be. *Stay aware of the consequences of your actions*, he told himself. Hours later, as he lay in bed, he searched for something pleasant to think about. Something calming that would allow sleep to come. He tried sports, then comedy movies...they didn't work. Finally, he found it: he visualised throwing his next petrol bomb.

12

REOPENING

Lucas emptied the smallest cabinet of three Seikos and four Casios before carrying it out back. The store was now less dingy and cluttered, although it verged on the minimalist. Having shifted things around, vacuumed, and dusted, the place was ready for new stock. He would spend some time on *mercadolibre* looking at current trends. As he put the Seikos and Casios in a bigger cabinet, a black Vostok Russian Military Diver watch caught his eye. He remembered getting it for a cheap price from an importer in Palermo. It wasn't an expensive watch, but the solidness and simplicity appealed to him now. He swapped it for the Seiko he'd been wearing the last few months, a watch with dials that looked cool and were next to useless.

Before he could open, he had to change Arquímedes's strap. The old sourpuss would be livid, Lucas had charged him eight hundred pesos but hadn't opened the store for weeks. It was surprising Arquímedes hadn't banged on the door in the middle of the night yet. His watch was a Chinese-made Lige, worth about thirty dollars. It had a blue face and gold-coloured bezel. The brand name wasn't appealing, but it looked OK and had lasted well. Lucas got the Lige out from under the counter, popped the spring bars, took off the broken black plastic strap, and chucked it in the bin. The new leather, Brazilian-made strap looked much smarter.

He opened at nine-thirty. Five minutes later, a woman came in with a boy of about ten. He wore a white coat that public schools used as a uniform. Lucas, who'd once worn one himself, thought the coats made kids look like little doctors. Why wasn't this kid in class? Maybe he and his mother had a real doctor's appointment. The woman's voluminous hair prevented Lucas from getting a good look at her face, so his eyes stayed on her thighs of a perfect thickness. After he had gazed a long time, she became self-conscious and peeled back her hair. He was relieved to find a fault: her eyes were too far apart, making her look like a fish. Unperturbed by his perving, she came over to the counter to buy a toy giraffe. The boy showed more interest in the cell phone cases, so it probably wasn't for him. After the mother and son, the customers kept coming. Next, a long haired *metalero* type drifted in, "I've never had a watch before," he claimed, "but we've got a gig on Saturday, and I'll need to know the time without looking at my phone." Lucas sold him a Casio. A man rubbing his red nose came in before lunch: "Got any fake Rolexes?" Lucas had five under the counter. Red nose bought two. In the afternoon, there were others, but no sign of Arquímedes.

He could go back to doing this, double his efforts to get watches at low prices. Unwanted stock from official outlets, deals online, bulk orders with importers – there were many ways to make small margins bigger. He'd be cleaner, dust more often, and wear a collared shirt. His father had wanted this: him to make a go of the business. It wasn't much to ask. He shouldn't try to be perfect though – he'd keep buying and selling stolen watches, without them he'd barely make rent.

The obstacle to his return to healthy living was the man upstairs. How to get rid of him? Pay him off? With what? Scare him? Difficult. Reason with him? Impossible. Lucas did have one vague idea... He'd read an article about a couple dying because of the gas heater in their bedroom. A stoppage in the supply of gas put out the flame. Later the gas came back on, but you had to light the flame manually on that type of heater. The couple was asleep and the door to their bedroom shut tight, the gas filled the room and poisoned them. A tragic accident. Something to work with! There was a wall heater like this in Gustavo's room. That bedroom had been Lucas's before his father died. His father had warned him about the heater many times. Lucas could interrupt the gas supply, but Gustavo would notice the flame going out and turn off the gas – he wasn't foolish enough to sleep with the heater on. There would be a way... On a warm night, Gustavo wouldn't use the heater; Lucas could sneak into the bedroom and turn the gas on! But when was the next warm night going to be? Never mind, he had to keep thinking. Whatever way he did it would be murder. Was he ready for this step? Perhaps he would be if something went wrong with their extorsion activities.

13

PIXIU

The target chino was on a corner. A rare occurrence, normally the Chinese didn't go for this more expensive real estate. While sizing up the scene, a pressure headache came on rapidly and affected his depth perception. From where he stood, the streets looked like diagonal lines with vanishing points on a two-dimensional screen. The dog walkers, ancient babble-mouths, and fast-walking young women travelled from the top of the screen diagonally to the bottom or vice versa. Passers-by looked across the intersection at him, noticing his expensive new Nikes. They knew where he'd got the money to buy them – and what he was up to now. Even the pregnant beggar, sitting outside the *panadería* eating yesterday's candy-hard bread, gave him a disapproving look. Lucas couldn't let them get to him. He took a deep breath and crossed the intersection diagonally. *Supermercado Fuxing, envíos a domicilio,* the sign said. Two Chinese kids, a toddler and his older sister, kicked a football around on the footpath out front. He hesitated. He didn't like it. These owners needed money for their kids. The football landed at his feet and he kicked it back to the smiling boy who could barely walk. Touching the ball helped make the flat-screen world 3D again.

Inside the supermarket, the man working the till, probably the owner of the place and father of the kids, was in conversation with a customer. They were talking about the Boca Juniors versus River Plate game coming up on Sunday. It was hard to feel xenophobic resentment against such a character. This didn't feel right at all. *Right? Since when had any of this been right?* Then he saw his way out. High on the wall, behind the counter, there was a small poster depicting a Chinese mythical creature. Gustavo's words came to him, "A pixiu is not unlike a xiezhi, but it doesn't have horns." Saved for now, his headache miraculously vanished as he exited the supermarket.

Gustavo, round the corner on his motorbike as usual, frowned when he heard the news. "Are you sure it wasn't a xiezhi?"

"Yeah, definitely no horns, not one. It's for the best, they had little kids."

"All these Chinese have kids, Lucas, why do you think there are so many of them? OK, get your phone out, let's take a look at the map."

Lucas had a photo of the wall map from the apartment on his phone. Gustavo zoomed in and squinted. "San Cristóbal, ten blocks, a green pin...a new place. Get on."

Five minutes later Lucas got off the bike again. Dodging dog shit, he made his way down the quiet street lined by struggling crown trees. The front of this chino was a mass of metal bars and handwritten signs: *milanesa de pollo 200 x kilo, pata y muslo 160 x kilo, queso cremoso 240 x kilo.* Lucas's stomach curled at the suggestion of raw chicken. Inside it was dark – he felt like he'd entered a cell. Maybe the store was so new they didn't have the lights connected yet. Enough sunlight came in the door in any case. The fridges buzzed away, confirming the place had electricity. Rather than the plasticy smell of most chinos, an odour of disinfectant floated in the air. This smell didn't encourage the buying of groceries, and there were no customers. Once again, Lucas couldn't be bothered with the spiel. He reached into his trouser pocket for the notice and unfolded the paper. It had a yellow dot in the corner: this was the renewal notice. He needed the notice for new stores with a green dot. Panic surged, but patting himself down he felt paper in his shirt pocket. The bent-over, wrinkled guy at the counter raised his eyebrows at Lucas's outstretched arm. "Take it, read it," Lucas said.

"One minute." The man opened and rattled around in several drawers under the counter.

"What are you doing?" Lucas felt his guts tensing; acid that tasted like Bolivian fried chicken came up his throat. *First the headache and now this. What is he reaching for?*

"My glasses...ah here they are." Lucas breathed out in relief. This wispy-haired, yellow-toothed gentleman was just old. He wasn't trying to antagonise. His almost-transparent skin perhaps couldn't bear electrical lights. With his glasses finally in place, he took the notice paper from Lucas. He read it and smiled, "Yes, I've been expecting you. Every store I've opened in Buenos Aires leeches have turned up. Now the boss doesn't even send Chinese to do the dirty work. Do you know what this paper says? Pay or we'll burn the store down. There'll be no need for that. You'll get your money. Now get the fuck out of my store. Go on. *¡Andate a la mierda!*"

This was a new experience for Lucas, a Chinese supermarket owner vocalising his contempt. He considered that the translucent old crank had been in Argentina too long and so bitched like a local. As they rode off, Lucas shouted at Gustavo's helmet, "Did you know the paper says we'll burn the store down in Chinese – is that a coincidence? Ping didn't know we were going to use Molotovs when she wrote the notices."

"It's a generic threat," Gustavo shouted back after pushing up his visor, "don't think too much."

14

BERSA 9MM

Gustavo parked behind a derelict car on a street where weeds broke through the tarmac and footpath tiles. The two-storey houses didn't reveal anything but brick, plaster, and barred windows. Beyond the Capital Federal, in Buenos Aires Province, but still within the city limits, thousands of streets looked like this one. He fumbled around in his leather backpack for his keys, then walked over to a green front door and unlocked it. Inside, light peeking through carelessly drawn curtains highlighted a thick cloud of dust in the air. His father sat in an armchair sleeping, the creases on his Klingon forehead no doubt filled with dust. Gustavo stood for a moment, then took a wad of pesos from his pocket and dropped it on the newspaper-covered coffee table.

Thinking this as good an opportunity as any, he went upstairs. The old man had the two-storey place to himself, luxury in this rabbit-warren city. Gustavo knew he didn't appreciate it – never having developed any hobbies, his bored and lonely father watched TV and slept. Upstairs in one of the three bedrooms was a chest of drawers for which only Gustavo had the keys. He ran his finger along the top of the chest, breaking the film of dust. A cleaner came once a week, but she knew the old man's habits: that he didn't come into this room and that his eyesight was shot. So she didn't bother dusting here. Gustavo wanted to go downstairs and get a cloth for the chest of drawers, but he'd have to vacuum too, and then his father would wake up... He unlocked and opened the second drawer down. Under two folded shirts, his fingers touched the cold metal of a Bersa 9mm – a locally made pistol generally thought of as reliable. He went back downstairs with the gun and out the back door. An iron-framed *parrilla* standing on a small expanse of dirt dominated the yard. It had seen action in its time – his father had been a butcher and put on a fantastic BBQ. Now it lay dormant. The lawn, once watered regularly, had died off. He could bury the gun here with no obvious trace. The yard was safe enough. If the gun was ever found, it would be too late. The shells found at the scene of the crime in Puerto Madero would be long forgotten, and the ballistics experts working on more important cases.

After burying the gun, he came inside, washed his hands, and sat down opposite his slumbering dad. Today's paper was on top of the large pile on the coffee table. The old man went without fail to get the newspaper from the kiosk down the road. More often than not, it was his only outing of the day. Gustavo picked up the paper and turned to the crime section to see the lead story.

'Vampire Farmworker Drinks Friend's Blood'

Now that, he reckoned, was a headline: something to make you forget whatever shocking crime happened the day before. He began to read:

'A twenty-three-year-old rural worker in Tucumán Province is charged with a brutal murder. Police arrested the man at five this morning after he stabbed to death a childhood friend and drank his blood. The accused confessed to the police, but claimed he acted in self-defence.

After the knifing, he went to a local bar in the town of San Ignacio and bought a bottle of whiskey. Back at the scene of the crime, he drank the whiskey mixed with his victim's blood.

Watching television and drinking on Sunday night, a disagreement began between the two men. The victim asked the accused to pass him a bottle of alcohol and the accused refused in a joking tone. Then the victim threw a chair at him.

According to a witness, after drinking the blood and whiskey, the man wanted to decapitate his friend and hang his head at the entrance to the property. Other workers dissuaded him from doing this. The accused went to bed, where police later found him. When asked why he wanted to drink the blood of his friend, he said it was because he was a deist. He claimed to believe in God, but he knew God wouldn't act if he did wrong. So why not see what it felt like?'

What a nut. That makes no sense, Gustavo said to himself. He wondered if his father had read the article: buying the newspaper every day didn't mean you read it. He chucked the paper back on the coffee table and went upstairs again.

***

After the shooting of the English couple in Puerto Madero, Gustavo had waited in a field near Ezeiza Airport. It was a place without cameras. Two of them arrived at midnight. The third Venezuelan, the original driver of the red Peugeot, being older and smarter, never surfaced. Gustavo went with the boys to a derelict house five minutes away. A colonel had lived there with his wife and children during the dictatorship. Legend had it the colonel tortured political prisoners in the basement. This seemed unlikely, as there were plenty of torture chambers to use in those days, why use the family home? With the return to democracy in '83 the military sold the house, but nobody wanted to live there. So the garden proved the perfect place to hide the Peugeot and the Suzuki motorcycle used in the robbery. Gustavo had briefed the boys on what to do in an emergency.

He first took the pistol, then their phones, but gave them new ones and more cash than they expected. He didn't want them angry – it was important they did what he told them. Their eyes were blank, maybe the kid who'd done the shooting had killed before. Maybe they both had. Gustavo guessed they'd been criminal minions since childhood, and along the way had all initiative knocked out of them. One was nineteen, the other twenty-one. "Get out of the country," he told them. As they got into the newly stolen VW he had ready for them, they were talking about going for pizza. Indeed, they looked very hungry. Gustavo knew they had a high chance of getting caught.

The English couple's suitcase lay on the backseat of the Peugeot. Inside, among the clothes, Gustavo found an iPad and an iPhone 11. They were brand new, although not in the original packaging. Lucas had picked well – Apple products were exorbitantly expensive in Argentina due to taxes, tariffs, and inflation. They sold for up to three times as much as in the United States or Europe.

Gustavo thought it unlikely the British couple was trying to make a buck selling the phone and iPad – more likely they were gifts for some local friends. Argentine customs were rapacious in charging import taxes, so this explained the lack of original packaging.

15

STEALING BUSES

He got the iPhone and iPad out of the third drawer in the chest. Flogging them through the usual channels, like a Facebook group, was still too risky even though the shooting happened two months ago. But he knew a place to get rid of them. With the electronics in his backpack, he went downstairs and sat on the sofa opposite the old man, who slept on. He'd always been like that: fast asleep at the drop of the hat, and then nothing would wake him until four-thirty in the morning – time to go to work. He never used an alarm clock either. Like his son, he was a small, wiry man. Apart from age, the major difference between the two was their hands. Gustavo had soft, unremarkable hands. His father's mitts were red and swollen with numerous scars.

In the papers, they'd debated the viability of robbing tourists arriving at the airport: a lot of risk and not much profit. Was the mastermind an idiot? In fact, it had been lucrative, but Gustavo didn't have much of the loot left. He imagined telling his dad about the Danish executive with dollars, euros, and kroners. He burnt the kroners without even checking the exchange rate. To know how much went up in smoke: that would have made him angry. The Venezuelans had jumped the Dane at a tollgate, a place traffic could have trapped them. "Why didn't you wait until the hotel?" he asked them. They had no answer. The Dane had a fake Submariner watch, strange given the cash and the quality of his clothes and suitcases.

Another success was the American. The boys acted late and nearly lost him when he entered an apartment building. The video that appeared in the press showed the American fiddling around in the foyer, having left a suitcase propping open the security door. Stupid. One of the boys went straight in and smacked him with the butt of the Bersa. That's what the pistol was for, to whack people, to point at people, not to shoot people. However, he could have hardly sent them out on jobs with a replica. The American had thousands of dollars' worth of jewellery for his Argentine sweetheart in his luggage.

Son, who are you doing this with? He imagined his father asking – if he asked anything. He had accepted his son was bad long ago, and then apparently hadn't given it any more thought.

Do you remember Javi, Dad?

Yes, his father smiled, *the kid who stole buses.*

Out of all the dreams eleven-year-old kids in Buenos Aires had, to be a bus driver was original, if banal. On his own initiative, Javi got on buses to sell small packets of serviettes. Most kids selling things on public transport came from a *villa miseria* – in that too Javi, who lived in the same neighbourhood as Gustavo, was an oddity. Javi watched the bus drivers carefully, fascinated by what they did. One day a fatso finished his shift and went into the terminal for a hamburger. "We leave the doors of our vehicles open," Fatso said in the police report. "We have an atmosphere of trust." Javi could hardly reach the pedals, but he was a natural at driving. He arrived at the school gates for the end of classes. Twelve kids took up his offer for a ride to the city centre. Gustavo was one of them. At a red light, someone spotted a child at the wheel of a city bus and rang the police. During the ensuing chase, Javi drove onto the footpath several times. It was a miracle he didn't hit any pedestrians. After, they put his photo up in the bus terminal – watch out for this character. Javi wanted his picture in the paper too, but his parents wouldn't allow it. Securing his legend early, he stole three more buses before he turned twelve. He was a skinny redheaded kid, but because of his achievements, nobody ever bullied him. By age twenty-five he was stocky and bald, but with the same cheeky grin. Nearly thirty years after his bus stealing heroics, Javi lived with his wife and daughter in Capital Federal, not far from Lucas's shop.

Because Javi's wife didn't like seeing Gustavo, they hatched their plans for the airport gang in the basement. Javi stole the cars and motorbikes used for the job. Gustavo got the plates from the triad. It was trouble driving through tollgates in a stolen car with its original plates. Sure, the barrier still went up when you paid, but then the technology alerted the police. Javi worked as the spotter, Gustavo dealt with the Venezuelans. Javi chose his targets on a whim – the Dane and American were hits, but they had flops too. A brief story appeared in the paper about the American getting bashed. Few people felt sorry for the rich Yankee. This was the gang's first appearance in the press and Javi, a narcissist needing attention, got excited. He showed the story to his wife. Of course, she blamed Gustavo for getting her husband involved in something like this.

And what's Javi up to now? He imagined his father leaning forward, keen to know.

Javi has disappeared. He told me he was off to Ciudad del Este. I know he had something going on selling counterfeit Samsung phones, a small-time operation. The phones came from Paraguay. He went up to buy some more and something happened. Maybe he's found a better gig up there.

The old man frowned, his forehead an impossibly complicated matrix of lines. *I don't think so, Javi is a nice kid...cares about others. He wouldn't abandon his wife and kid. Have you gone round to talk to his wife?*

She doesn't like me.

Your friend could be in trouble up there. Ciudad del Este can be a dangerous place. Maybe you could help, but you lack empathy, Gustavo.

You've been telling me that since I was a kid, that and not much else. In any case, I don't need Javi anymore.

16

VILLA

Nothing moved on the street, apart from a man smoking a cigarette in front of the kiosk a few doors down. Gustavo knew him as the grey-haired owner of that little shop. A character who smoked a pack a day, never got sick, and never took a day off. But one day not far off, sure as inflation, he'd drop dead of a heart attack. As much as this guy liked to work, he'd lock the kiosk up tight before dark. Gustavo had known a time here with more life. On the corner, there had been a security booth, manned by a Paraguayan with a walkie-talkie. He couldn't remember his name now. As kids, they'd loved to throw things at him. One day the booth was gone. The residents couldn't afford it anymore. Then a child was run over, a house got broken into, someone was shot – residents made their homes more secure. People in this neighbourhood had jobs, paid taxes, this was far from being a *villa miseria* with teenagers smoking crack, but people started avoiding going out when they could.

As he rode back into the city the idea his father hadn't been breathing nagged at him. He didn't plan on visiting again for a while. If the old man was dead would anybody realise? The kiosk guy? Then the gun might be discovered too soon. No, this was silly. His dad was on his last legs but still breathing.

He crossed over the Alsina Bridge back into the Capital Federal and parked on a side street off Avenida Sáenz. His destination wasn't a place for his Kawasaki and, despite the cold, he left his leather jacket locked under the bike seat. At the intersection at the end of Sáenz, he waited at a pedestrian crossing. The white stripes marking the crossing were barely visible. It was doubtful they'd be re-painted soon in this part of town. Cars and trucks hurtled through the intersection with no thought of stopping for pedestrians; it looked like dangerous work to get across. Safely on the other side, he passed a small *parrilla*, where unsavoury characters ate *choripanes* under the watchful eyes of street dogs and oil-slick pigeons. The *choripanes* didn't look appetising, but his stomach rumbled and he regretted not eating before beginning this mission. Turning the corner, he was confronted by stairs leading up to the Alsina Bridge. The 1930s structure, with an Ottoman palace-style façade painted white and gold, straddled the river between the neighbourhood of Nueva Pompeya and the District of Lanus. It occurred to him he could come back and drop the gun off the bridge at night. How deep was the unmoving sludge below the bridge? Maybe it wasn't such a great idea, it looked too much like a place to dump a murder weapon.

Half a block from the steps was the entrance of Villa 303, the ad hoc brick structures of a shantytown instantly recognisable. A few kids were playing football in the dirt in front of these precarious brick dwellings. Several mangy dogs sniffed Gustavo's feet as he entered this 'unofficial' part of the city.

"Hey, kid...Nico here?" Gustavo addressed a skinny boy of about twelve.

"Yes, I'll get him." The kid ran off and disappeared into a house. Gustavo noticed he had something wrong with his hips. The way he ran suggested a lack of concern about the problem. A squat man in a Boca shirt and jeans emerged from the house, wonky hips right behind him. The man smiled at Gustavo and offered his hand.

"How are you, I'm Nico. You called earlier. Gustavo, isn't it? Let's see what you have for me."

Gustavo took off his backpack, rummaged around, and produced the iPad and iPhone. Nico, thumbs stuck in his belt under a generous beer gut, offered a faint smile.

"Nice backpack, is that real leather?"

Gustavo felt his forehead corrugating. "It is, got it cheap on a trip out to the pampas a couple of months ago, stitching is already coming apart."

"Too bad, I like the look of it... Do you have the chargers?"

"Yes, I do."

"Come inside and have a beer then."

Gustavo walked out of the villa with fifteen thousand pesos. He could have got forty thousand on Facebook. In the villa, it was take it or leave it.

At Sáenz and Caseros, he weaved between cars to get to the front of the queue at the lights. At the white line, he put his foot on the tarmac and waited for the red light to change. A bump jolted him – the car behind had moved forward and not braked in time. The nudge was soft. Had it been done on purpose? Gustavo struggled to silence the anger that beat in him like a drum. He could not see the driver's face in the rear view. He imagined a man on the edge, calculating that only by making another explode he could save himself. "Necochea," Gustavo said to himself out loud. He took a deep breath, "Necochea." The light turned green.

When his father did die, Gustavo planned to move to the seaside city of Necochea. A hundred thousand dollars would buy a small hotel there. His father's house, in the neighbourhood it was in, would sell for a fraction of that.

One summer, over a decade ago, he drove down the Atlantic coast until he reached Necochea's beachside avenue lined by high-rises. During the days, he wandered the acres of yellow sand where holidaymakers set up umbrellas and canvas sun shelters. La Frontera disco occupied his nights, after preparing in his hotel room with a twenty-peso bottle of vodka. The club, a big shed on the beach, became busy after two in the morning. Once inside, bad tequila shots punched the liver and made things happen. Many times in Buenos Aires without a friend to call on, he had gone out drinking alone. It always felt awkward and ended badly. Not in Necochea, he was one of the crowd there.

The parents of the girl he met at La Frontera had passed away. The no parents-in- law jewel, imagine how easy life with her could have been! The good news continued: she was quiet and never disagreed with him. She didn't say his eyes scared her, that he was insipid or empty, things other girls had told him. Pretty but not perfect, the dark skin on her abdomen had white splotches, as if she had Michael Jackson's skin disease. She lived with her aunt and did cleaning for a family with kids who were spoiled pains-in-the-arse. She was twenty-two, he was twenty-six. Stupidly, he left. Not enough money, too much alcohol, being young and wanting to move on...weak reasons. Nothing had gone right since. He was too old for La Frontera now and the girl wouldn't be around, but he believed positive things would happen if he went back down the coast. Thinking about Necochea after visiting his father was a good result because seeing the old man usually stirred up bad memories. However, going to the villa – a place where bad things can happen – had made him tense. A little trip to Puerto Madero would relax him, provided he could stay in control. No, it would be better to go back to the shop, have something to eat and plan for the next Chinese supermarket. But when the turnoff came, he didn't take it.

17

PINCERS

He rode past the hotel in Puerto Madero where the British couple had been shot. He didn't notice, didn't think of it. The illegal casinos in Puerto Madero came and went, some got busted, others disappeared for no obvious reason. Gustavo had lost money in all of them. It had been worth it, because in these casinos you made connections. Any petty criminal could better themselves here – Gustavo had picked up jobs as security for businessmen afraid to go to nightclubs alone, and found out the triads could get you duplicate number plates. He was finished with blackjack, roulette, and the one arm bandits, not because of losing money, but because he'd played them too many times. The dopamine release was stingy even with a win. One casino, however, was offering something new. He'd tried it once, a bizarre experience, and he wanted to do it again.

He rapped on the metal door of a warehouse-style building. A thick neck in a suit opened and gave him a nod. Inside three middle-aged couples crowded around a blackjack table, their faces sweaty masks of concentration under the unsuitably bright lights. The teenage croupier had drops running down his forehead too. Beside the table was a tall gas heater usually used for outside bars, the health and safety inspector didn't do the rounds of these places. Past the blackjack table was a roulette wheel bereft of patrons and beyond that an expanse of concrete floor. He walked across this space to a reception booth staffed by a woman in a navy blazer and satin blouse. "Welcome sir," she said, flashing brilliant teeth. "Wait a minute please, they are fighting now." Around one metre seventy-five tall, with jutting cheekbones and long blond hair, she was quite something. Not anybody could work in a place like this. He sat on a black leather sofa and tried not to stare. Two minutes later, she put her hand over her earpiece, concentrating. "They are done now sir. You can go in."

The dimly lit room with faded carpet had once been the staff canteen. The barman, in a waistcoat and bowtie, served him a weak fernet. Madonna was on high volume, an eighties number from the soundtrack of a film starring Christopher Walken and Sean Penn. He struggled to re-member the name of the movie. A circle marked by black tape dominated the middle of the room – around it half a dozen middle-aged men, drinks in hands, talked up a storm. They were either politicians or lawyers. No, their bodies were in ruinous shape, so definitely politicians, Gustavo reckoned. Lawyers were vain and they went to the gym. Beyond the group, a tuxedo-clad white-haired man in his sixties cleared his throat and spoke into a microphone: "Gentlemen, no ladies present I'm afraid, although we welcome one newcomer," he nodded towards Gustavo, "let me explain a little about what we do here." Gustavo groaned inwardly, he'd heard this last time. "In a minute you will be introduced to *Tityus trivittatus*, the most deadly scorpion in Argentina, but first a few details." The politicians must have heard this story minutes ago, but they were skilled at blocking out what they didn't want to hear. "The scorpions may run rather than fight. You will be safe in your shoes, don't panic and don't stand on the scorpions unless you want to pay for them. Our scorpions come from the Centre of Animal Venoms in Catamarca. They also provide antidotes, so that covers us for accidents. The scorpion has been around for three hundred and fifty million years. We have them under control here, however, I have a feeling they'll be around long after the extinction of *Homo sapiens*. Notice gentlemen the dehumidifiers on the wall. Scorpions don't like the damp and we want them to be in fighting shape." The man sounded like a demented schoolteacher. Drunk gamblers must have been a more compliant captive audience than kids.

"Here they are, our two combatants."

The blond had entered with a box balanced on each palm. Gustavo and the others crowded around her. Through the transparent lids, he could see a scorpion in each box. One was slightly larger. That was enough. He placed a bet of three hundred dollars with the schoolteacher. The lights went out. He heard the woman's quick high-heeled retreat. Two fluorescent scorpions stood facing each other in the circle. Nobody knows why scorpions glow under UV light, but finally capitalism had found a way of taking advantage of this oddity. The tail of the bigger scorpion struck out but misjudged the range and missed. The smaller arachnid moved around and grabbed the flank of its enemy with both pincers, perfect positioning to drive its sting between two plates of abdominal armour. The glow-in-the-dark death throes were brief.

After it was over and the lights were up, the blond woman approached him. "What did you think, sir?" she asked. "The big guy didn't seem to know how to use his pincers, did he?"

"No."

He knew she was trying to keep him there. The politicians had each other, but he was alone and likely to leave after one lost bet. "I'll go for the next two, you'll be here, right?"

"What?" The guy behind the bar had turned Madonna back on, louder than before. "I wish they'd play some Argentine music in here, something in Spanish at least."

"You don't like Madonna?"

"I can't hear you."

"The scorpions," she yelled in his ear, "I'm going to get two new ones. The winner of this round takes a rest. They only fight once a night" She gave him her great smile. This time he saw lipstick smudged on her teeth. He guessed she offered extra services – not within his budget though.

He lost again, won once, and then lost three times. He was twelve hundred down. This was against the odds, true bad luck, and then it occurred to him the fights could be rigged. He hadn't been paying attention to the politicians. Were they winning? Could they be ring-ins: invertebrates betting on invertebrates? He wanted to bust their faces but willed himself to walk out the door. The invertebrates, sooner or later, always won. Wait. They wouldn't win if he still had the Bersa pistol. A great opportunity, politicians leaving an illegal casino with stacks of cash, they wouldn't want that in the press. With no complaint to police, they wouldn't check the cameras. The perfect crime, but you couldn't ride around Buenos Aires with a pistol on you waiting for such a rare chance. Well, you could if you trusted your temper. It was now dark outside and cold. Gustavo didn't put his jacket on right away though; rage kept him hot. For a horrible moment, he couldn't remember where he'd parked his bike. Twelve hundred dollars was a lot of money, but no problem, Lucas could take up the slack. The one thing he could control: Lucas, a passive creature. Although the way he'd thrown that Molotov had impressed. Together they were going to make a lot of money from extorting Chinese supermarkets. Necochea might not be so far off. A little calmer now, he remembered his hunger and rode up the hill to the microcentro.

He parked a block away from the pizzeria. On Avenida Corrientes, he dodged through pedestrian dawdlers looking up at theatre show billboards. On these advertisements, men wore top hats and hideous smiles, and women displayed glitter-covered silicon breasts that almost burst out of the 2D format. Rubbish shows, Gustavo could not imagine who went. In the packed pizzeria, no table was available for a solo diner. He had to stand at the counter with lonely old men and exhausted workers shaking oregano onto measly slices of *muzzarella*, but nothing else would get to him tonight. Famished, he ate an entire pizza *napolitana* topped with half a kilo of cheese.

After, feeling better, he ordered a cup of red wine. He had faith that his digestion would handle all this. It was time to give himself a pep talk. The most important thing? Give up casinos. He had always been willing to gamble on anything. It started at eight years old when he bet a friend twenty pesos he could eat a cockroach and lost. The horrible chemical the bug used to ward off predators still came back to him in times of stress. A hint of it materialised in his mouth now, he gulped at his wine to get rid of it. *Scorpions, politicians, and cockroaches: an evening of invertebrates*, he said to himself. And he almost managed a smile.

18

RAID

The press proved unusually perceptive in its analysis of the political background to the crackdown on the Xiezhi Triad. Large supermarket chains, most notably Carrefour, were threatening to leave the country. Due to the economic situation consumption was down, and Carrefour and friends claimed they couldn't survive without a tax break, an idea the government quashed outright. Then they pointed the finger at their competitors, the Chinese supermarkets: those famed tax evaders had fifteen percent of the market. By not paying tax, they could keep their prices low. In addition, none of their employees signed contracts, and so had little protection from the labour laws. The president agreed that these were big problems.

"We are going to take action. You need to start respecting the laws of this country," he declared, playing hardball during a meeting with the Chamber of Argentine and Asian Retailers. The Chinese businessmen representing this legitimate organisation fought back. "Firstly," their spokesman said, "the idea that none of the thousands of Chinese supermarkets pay tax is false, it's based purely on prejudice. Secondly, there is some evasion, but taxes will be easier to pay if the government does something about triad extortion. The Chinese community sees taxes as just another form of extortion, Mr President, and the triads are more dangerous than the government, so their claims come first. What are the police doing to shut these triads down, sir? Nothing! The police have turned a blind eye from the time Chinese supermarkets started opening up in Argentina twenty-five years ago. In the last five years alone, fifty-seven mafia attacks have terrorised Chinese supermarkets and twenty-one people, either owners or employees, have been killed. The police haven't charged anyone in relation to these deaths. How is this possible, Mr President?" The president turned green for a moment, his aides hadn't warned him that the Chamber of Argentine and Asian Retailers would be this prepared and fierce.

Duly admonished, the country's leader changed his focus from the downtrodden supermarket owners to the triads. It was true the police had been lax in investigating the Chinese mafia – they saw them as more hassle than they were worth. It was hard to get a decent translator to monitor them. They communicated in a number of dialects and members of the local Chinese community couldn't be coerced into translating. Also, when the triads got violent it was kept within their own community, and this the police respected. Apart from extortion, the triads' other big racket was bringing counterfeit goods over the border from Ciudad del Este in Paraguay. The police would have to coordinate with the Paraguayan authorities to do anything about this, again too much hassle.

The president was somewhat nervous about calling the Chinese embassy, but his aides urged him to. They admitted that in the past the Chinese government had flat out denied the presence of triads in Argentina and might do it again, "But it's worth a try, sir." The call turned out better than anyone expected. The Chinese ambassador was happy to hear from the president and agreed to send no less than a small group of People's Liberation Army translators to help get information about triad criminal activities.

The Chinese had changed their tune due to the recent détente between Argentina and the People's Republic of China – the longstanding row concerning anti-dumping tariffs imposed on Chinese products was over. Last month China had made its goodwill known by signing a contract to import hundreds of millions of tons of Argentine soy. Furthermore, the Asian giant committed to providing technical support to the Bartolomé Díaz oil exploration project that the Argentines had been struggling to get off the ground. Now they were going to help bust the triads. Police started sending the recordings of phone calls between triad members to the PLA translators. In no time, they had the information they needed to launch an anti-triad operation, which they dubbed "Panda's Heart." The president was satisfied that this would be a PR coup; the papers loved writing about the mysterious triads, and stories about proactive policing would dampen down his reputation as being soft when it came to law and order.

Panda's Heart kicked off with a crack team of federal police assembling outside the building where Ping's restaurant was located. They had come ready in black uniforms, helmets, and body armour. Half the squad had SIG Sauer semi-automatic rifles. The cops climbed the stairs to the fifth floor and entered the empty dining hall. In the kitchen, they relieved Chef Li of his cleaver. At the back of the kitchen, a locked metal door stopped their progress – according to police information, the room on the other side contained a shitload of contraband. To keep the element of surprise, they used an explosive rather than a battering ram to break the door. Once the smoke cleared, the officers entered in formations of four, made up of two riot-shield bearers and two shooters. The Chinese gangsters were waiting for them. Bullets zinged off the shields and one cop took a body armour hit. Ping's men were outnumbered and outgunned. Taking a bullet in the leg, floppy-fringed Juan dropped to the floor. A second triad soldier took a hit in the leg, another in the shoulder. That was enough. The Chinese put down their guns with the triad's honour still intact.

Photos in the paper showed officers with blurred faces standing next to stacks of contraband: cigarettes and electronics that ranged from fake Sony tablets to hairdryers. They also seized a substantial number of handguns. Not present to enjoy the fun, Ping was later arrested at her residence in the posh neighbourhood of Olivos wearing pyjamas. The press was excited that she lived not five blocks from the presidential *quinta*.

Initially, Ping found herself in a holding cell that smelled strongly of urine. Politically and spatially, the cell was divided: two stocky Peruvian women stood on one side and three willowy Argentines on the other. A compact Chinese woman thrown in the middle was an unknown factor. The newcomer could be an ally, or someone to prey on. Experience told Ping if she kept silent it would take the others time to figure her out. The cell did have toilet paper, and she twisted a couple of sheets up tightly and stuck them in her nose. She needed to pee but preferred to explode than use the shared toilet bowl.

When the evening meal arrived, Ping spoke to the guard, who, at the mention of money, was all ears. She lent Ping her cell phone to make the bank transfers. Fifteen minutes later, Ping moved to a private cell – which, importantly, had its own toilet. A visit from the boss's lawyer followed this welcome change of environment. A young guy with spiky hair in a flashy suit, Pablo Zheng was a graduate of the University of Buenos Aires. The prestigious public university didn't charge fees, but Pablo hadn't said no to financial support from Ping when he was a student. He didn't like to remember what he did for her in return. Back then, he'd been skinny and much to her taste, now he weighed ninety kilograms, worked out obsessively, and ate more red meat than a fully-grown puma. People who had known him a long time laughed because he'd been into instant noodles and video games as a kid. Born in Argentina, the Fujianese language he'd picked up from his parents was ropey. Sometimes Pablo had to use Spanish to express himself, especially when it came to legal conversations. This annoyed Ping because using dialect was a defence against eavesdroppers. Pablo could be trusted though.

"Has A-Dong from the Pixiu Triad been arrested?"

"No boss, apparently he made arrangements with the police before this went down. The government and police only needed to bust one triad to look good."

"That Cantonese scumbag... Are they onto our extortion activities as well?"

"Yes, getting the contraband gave them momentum, and now they are looking carefully at the tapes of the explosion in the supermarket in Parque Patricios. Make sure the police don't get hold of the guys who did that. Remember they aren't part of the community and can be used against you. Don't disappear them either, it would be risky at the moment. Get them to safety, you've got a few days."

"Maybe I should have stuck with Chinese who wouldn't talk no matter what. A shame this is happening now. Those guys were getting payments. I didn't want our people doing the dirty work anymore."

"It was a great idea, boss – you're a victim of the new political climate, bad timing that's all."

Back in the cell, Ping sat down on the hard mattress and considered the graffiti on the wall. Amongst all the usual filth, one phrase stood out: "I'm your nemesis because I know you." Of all the former occupants of the cell, it was a decent bet that the author of this sentence had been the only philosopher. Ping could do with talking to her nemesis, A-Dong, boss of the Pixiu Triad. He was an enemy, but on the same level as Ping. He knew her world well, and so was somebody she could talk to. Occasionally, in times of truce, they met to discuss importing foodstuffs and other business. A good storyteller, A-Dong had told Ping his family in China was very poor. To make his way in the world, he had caught a bus to Guangzhou on his seventeenth birthday. The city breathed the dust of the construction boom – you couldn't see buildings fifty metres away. It was better to smoke an unfiltered cigarette than inhale that air. Construction work was easy to get, but conditions terrible. A-Dong and the other workers slept on the footpath outside the building site. The foreman fed them but stalled on paying wages. He told them to be patient. The other workers, mostly under thirty but with old men's creases in their faces, took this stoically. Not content to wait around, A-Dong and another young guy attacked the foreman with spades and knocked him out cold. He had five thousand yuan in cash on him, an amount that would have gone a long way to paying the workers' wages. A-Dong and his friend almost drank themselves to death that night. Great times... When he himself ended up working as a foreman, A-Dong was always careful and paid a couple of thugs to protect him. He saved money and bought a ticket to Argentina. This was a stepping-stone, his long-term aim was the USA, where real money could be made. It turned out that he made decent money in Argentina and the USA never happened...

The key turned in the lock, interrupting Ping's reverie. "Get up," the guard said. "Come with me, someone wants to talk to you."

19

ILLEGAL FISHING

A surprise waited in the interview room. Ping had expected the Argentine police, but in the windowless room, a Chinese woman sat at a square table with two glasses of water on it. Ping didn't know that this was one of the PLA 'translators' sent to help take down the triads. *Who is she? Why didn't Pablo mention this?* A chasm of fear opened up in Ping's stomach. *She must be from the Chinese government.* Standing up, the woman offered Ping her hand and the boss felt like a dwarf. The government liked tall army personnel, especially for overseas missions. Despite the heating inside the room, the woman wore a black woollen jumper. It didn't reveal much except that her shoulders were more developed than most Chinese women. She had the face of somebody always in the right, even when they were wrong. Another sort of personality in her position might fear making the wrong step and have a haunted expression. Not this one, Ping could feel it. Here was a person who would be the trusted mouthpiece of the behemoth she represented, no matter what kind of doublethink was required. The woman gestured for Ping to take a seat, sat down herself, and noisily cleared her throat. Knowing the interview was about to begin, Ping instinctively moved her own chair back from the table, but there was nowhere to go.

"How are you being treated, compatriot?"

"Well, thank you." Ping was going to be cautious and polite. Normally, she liked the sound of her own voice, but now she should watch and listen. "How should I address you?"

"Call me María. You don't need my Chinese name. I'm here to tell you about something you can do for your country...something that will help you get out of this situation."

"And what is that, María?" Ping asked, inching her chair forward.

"Have you heard about the attack on a Chinese fishing vessel off Mar del Plata last year? And how the Chinese government showed great restraint in not punishing this insult?"

María pronounced 'sh' like a Fujianese, but she spoke in Mandarin instead of dialect. Ping guessed she did this to maintain her distance.

"I don't keep up with current affairs much," Ping said, shrugging her shoulders.

Annoyance flashed across María's face, but her voice was steady. "The Argentine coast guard attacked the fishing boat, *Lan Hai,* because of its...alleged illegal fishing for squid in Argentine waters. The coastguard hailed the *Lan Hai* by loudspeaker, but the Chinese crew didn't understand and fled. The Argentines gave chase and started shooting at the *Lan Hai*'s hull until it sank. They picked the crew out of the water, and have subsequently allowed most back to China, apart from two, who – we are not sure why – the Argentines think are Chinese Communist Party officials. Are you following me?"

Ping's head had begun spinning. *Politics, I'm in deep now – deep waters.* The thought made her giggle.

"What are you laughing at, Ping? Your freedom depends on this. We can have the Argentines throw away the key."

Ping took a long drink of water. She had heard about the huge fleet of Chinese fishing vessels that often invaded Argentine waters and knew the coast guard didn't have the resources to stop them. But Communist Party officials on a fishing boat? That sounded suspicious. Maybe the coast guard sank the *Lan Hai* because it wasn't there to fish at all. Ping knew asking these questions would be pointless. She should cooperate, pay whatever amount they wanted – obviously this was about money. The Communist Party trumped the triads in the gangster stakes. It wouldn't hurt to play dumb for a while longer though.

"OK, what do you want me to do? I don't follow. Cut to the chase, please."

"You have to be somewhere?" María snapped without humour. "The new government here in Argentina is more cooperative than the last one and using back channels we have come to an agreement for the release of the two officials...er, that is crew members...but there is a snag. Argentina is a corrupt country, and the Chinese government doesn't pay bribes. This is where you come in, a woman of your means. Do as we say, and you can go free."

Ping swallowed – the bribe for the release of two party cadres would be hefty.

"This doesn't make any sense. You don't pay bribes. I get that. But surely you have to pay a bribe to get me released. Or maybe you don't need to pay? If you can get a triad boss released without paying you can get the officials released without paying."

María smiled. She was almost beautiful Ping observed with gloom.

"They are crew members, not officials. No, you don't get it: we can have you put in prison forever without paying anything. If you pay the bribe for the crew members, we won't pull those strings. Then you can pay for your own release... Goodbye citizen Ping, take heart you are helping two of your compatriots. Even a bad egg like you can aid the motherland. When you're ready, tell the guards you can make the payment. They know who to contact."

Ping hadn't felt so humiliated in a long time. Back in her cell, she sat down on the mattress and stared at the wall again. The phrase scrawled there, "I'm your nemesis because I know you," had taken on new meaning.

20

THE CONVENT

Sitting up in bed, Ping poured herself a cup of green tea from the pot. She wore pink flannelette pyjamas with cats on them. Her hair was tied back tightly as usual. On the other side of the bed, his head propped up by a couple of pillows, Juan was smoking, an ashtray balanced on his sunken chest. Shirtless, his ribs were remarkable. Taking a sip of tea and swallowing, Ping became aware of her jaw clenching. She concentrated on relaxing it, but a phone call interrupted her.

"*Wei*...Pablo?"

"*Wei*, boss...bad news..."

"What?"

"Another cache of contraband raided and confiscated."

"Again...what is going on here? Isn't the government satisfied with their crackdown? They've looked good in the media. I paid a big bribe to get out... And they still won't leave us alone?"

"The government is happy, but the police smell blood...meaning profit. With the government's attention elsewhere, they can sell our contraband themselves. But where are they getting their info from boss?"

"All our guys are out of jail?"

"Yes."

"You better come over to Olivos, Pablo." Ping hung up and got to her feet. "Get dressed now," she said to Juan, "and in the future don't smoke in my bed, it reeks."

Pablo Zheng arrived at Ping's house an hour later. Juan opened the door, and Pablo followed the boss's limping lover into the kitchen. Juan still had a bandage on his leg, covering the flesh wound he'd received in the shootout with the police. Apart from a wok sitting on one of the burners, it could have been any Argentine kitchen. Under the four-burner gas cooktop was an oven pristine from lack of use. Jars of *yerba*, teabags, and sugar sat on the bench, the kettle had a setting that brought the water to ninety degrees, the ideal temperature for mate. The spices, if there were any, must have been hiding away in the cupboards. The boss, now wearing a polo shirt and navy trousers, gestured for Pablo to sit down and waved Juan off to smoke his cigarettes elsewhere. Pablo had rushed over, he was still in his Adidas jacket and gym shorts. His hair was without gel. Ping cast a disapproving eye at his well-developed quads. He could have used a glass of water but the boss didn't offer him one. "Well, Pablo, what do you know?"

"As I said on the phone, I don't know who gave the police the location. Fang perhaps, he's still in hospital, anyone can get to him: the Pixiu Triad or the police."

"Who is Fang?"

"You're kidding, boss. One of your men, shot in the raid on the restaurant."

"Ah, OK."

"What about Juan? Aren't you, um...intimate with him. Does he know anything he shouldn't?"

"He's been to all our contraband storage places if that's what you mean, it's part of his job...it wasn't him."

"It's not the police finding more contraband I'm worried about, what about your cash, boss? I'm sure they will sniff it out soon. Now is time to move it."

"Where to though, Pablo? The last government virtually dug up the whole country looking for hidden treasure. Where is safe now? Who is offering a place?"

"Let me find out. I've heard there are new people on the scene willing to play bank."

***

It was early, very early. Ping sat in the passenger seat of the HiAce van, the whites of her eyes injected with blood and the lids puffy. An assault rifle sat across her lap. Gustavo was driving and Pablo sat in the back with the money. The lawyer was rubbing his hands together, possibly to indicate they hurt. Ping had made him dig up the money. She was still pissed at him for not warning her about the woman working for the Chinese government. Pablo already knew about the money, but why bring Gustavo along? *Still acting on my whims too much*, Ping told herself, *I'm impulsive, far from the perfect boss*. Or maybe it had been wise? Gustavo would make the nuns more comfortable, and that was important. He was calm too, driving nice and slowly.

They arrived at five in the morning. Gustavo jumped out, ignored the chance to appreciate the starry sky, and opened the sliding door of the HiAce. Pablo passed out two maroon suitcases, each weighing twenty-six kilograms. The wheels started rattling loudly as Gustavo rolled the cases up the stone path. "Carry them," Ping hissed after him. She held her breath. Had the sound woken the neighbours? "Get in the driver's seat," she ordered Pablo, who sulkily obeyed. "We'll be back soon." Rifle held diagonally across her torso, she hurried after Gustavo. Fifty metres on was a stone building. Ping rang the front doorbell and they waited. She started shivering...they waited some more. Finally, the door opened. An elderly nun peered out at them. She was wearing a brown dress and black habit with a white stripe – maybe putting on the habit and dress had caused the delay. Surely, nuns were up at this time of the morning though. The outer security door of metal bars remained shut.

"Who are you, and what are you doing here at this hour?"

"We have an arrangement with Sister Elva," Ping answered.

"What?"

"Sister Elva, we came to see her."

"I'll go talk to her." The nun shuffled off.

"I suppose she's playing it safe making us wait like this," Ping commented. Gustavo didn't say anything.

A couple of minutes later the nun was back. Instead of inviting them in, she opened the metal door and came out. "Follow me." They went around the back of the building. Ping guessed they were in a garden, perhaps an orchard. The suitcases couldn't be rolled over the mass of twigs and fallen leaves – Gustavo lifted them using his strong shoulders. A sensor light turned on and a small chapel appeared in front of them. The sister unlocked the padlock and drew back the bolt. The hinges of the solid wooden doors creaked. "Nobody will look in here," she said with a conspiratorial grin that doubled her wrinkles. She must have been close to eighty.

"That's what we are paying you for," Ping said, but the nun didn't seem to hear. "Roll up the carpet," she said to Gustavo. Underneath was a wooden floor. The sister knelt to push an invisible latch and opened a trap door. "Give me a hand up, young man...thank you... Have you got the money vacuum packed? We can't guarantee this won't get damp in winter."

"Yes, yes, we have, thank you."

Gustavo placed the suitcases in the vault, closed it, and rolled the carpet out. *All set*, Ping thought, *time to get out of here*. Their host had other ideas,

"Sister Elva would like to see you before you go."

"Is that necessary? I have the envelope for you right here."

"She likes to see the faces of the people she's helping out."

Ping could understand this: it was a wise move to meet your clients in person. They retraced their steps to the front of the stone house. The sister showed them into a living room with a large crucifix on the wall. Ping and Gustavo perched on uncomfortable wooden chairs while the sister went off to get Elva. The one plush red armchair looked inviting, but Ping and Gustavo left it alone – they had good instincts about hierarchy in underworld organisations.

Sister Elva was closer to ninety than eighty. She wore a habit, a green woollen jersey, and a long skirt. The younger nun held her right elbow and wrist, guiding her in. She deposited Elva in the red armchair but didn't sit down herself. "Make some tea, Lucia, do we have any biscuits?" Elva's voice was surprisingly strong and clear of croak.

"Yes, we do, Elva."

Tea? Ping saw Gustavo's face fall, he wanted to get out of there too. She tried to think of an excuse to leave but couldn't come up with anything. *Shit, the neighbours will be up soon, and Pablo will freak out.* The SIG Sauer 516 rifle lay across her knees. Quite a piece of equipment, it now made her feel ridiculous.

"It's a positive thing you are doing." Elva was looking at Gustavo.

"Thank you, sister," he said without feeling.

"The money you are paying us will be used well. That will help your soul, because what you put in our vault you didn't earn. How did you get it? Go ahead, tell me and you'll feel better."

"We sold some property and don't trust the bank with our money, sister," Ping said, realising how unbelievable this sounded.

The nun looked briefly at Ping and then back to Gustavo. "I'm sorry, what did your friend say?" Ping realised that her Chinese face meant she couldn't be understood here. Maybe this was for the best.

"That we won it gambling," Gustavo said in a flat voice.

Good enough, Ping thought.

Lucia returned with a tray of tea, chocolate biscuits, and *tostadas de mesa*. She put it down on the coffee table, next to the copy of *Time* magazine with the Pope's face on the cover. Ping took a biscuit and a sip of tea. She tried not to make a face – one thing she had never got used to in Argentina was their tea. Gustavo blew on his tea. Elva put three sugars in hers. "Do you need anything else, Elva?" Lucia asked.

"No dear, you can go." '

Ping reached for another biscuit.

"I'm glad to see your foreign friend likes our humble tea and biscuits," Sister Elva said smiling. Encouraged, Ping took a knife and scooped up some butter, which spread on a piece of toast like a dream. Lucia had warmed it – impressive. Elva began to prattle about renovations around the convent; she had some big plans. Gustavo nodded and gave the odd monosyllabic answer. The old nun didn't seem concerned about the rifle. Ping wondered what kind of crooks had visited the convent before. It bothered her.

After drinking their tea and saying awkward goodbyes to the nuns, they walked back to the van to find Pablo fast asleep. Back in Olivos, Ping herself took a nap – it had been a very early morning. Two hours later she woke up, and while many would have been groggy after such a mid-morning sleep, the boss was clear-minded. Her eyes were no longer puffy and bloodshot, but the question of who else banked with nuns still bugged her, Pablo might not have been smart enough to check. After making tea in the proper way, she called him.

"*Wei*, boss."

"*Wei*, Pablo. How many vaults do you think they have at the convent?"

"We didn't see a tenth of their grounds. You know the Catholic Church has land to burn."

"So they have a lot of clients. Where did you hear about them? The nuns I mean. Another lawyer?"

"Yes, boss. Guido Saavedra, he's a top defence lawyer."

"Damn, Pablo...that's not great news. Get me a list of clients Saavedra's defended in the last two years and email it...today."

When she got the list, Ping scanned through the names. Her tight face went pale when she recognised a name on the list. Everyone knew that name. She got on the phone to Pablo again.

"Check out sisters Elva and Lucia, where their family members are and what they do."

"Boss, what's up? Who's on the list?"

"None other than Hernández the Artist: the greatest currency forger of all time. What if we withdraw a bunch of fake notes from the vault in a year and the nuns say they know nothing about it?"

"So we've got to let them know we can hurt them? I get it. Always thinking – that's why you are the boss."

"Family, Pablo, we need to get to their families, these old religious girls would have no problem becoming martyrs themselves." Ping hung up the phone satisfied, there was nothing like doing your job well. Then she remembered an order from Ciudad del Este that needed cancelling. Shit, she should have done it yesterday. *To business...always to business*.

21

CHINCHULINES

"Too much sugar, but decent for one hundred pesos don't you think?" Gustavo asked and Lucas nodded his agreement. The two men sat on plastic chairs outside a hole-in-the-wall bar drinking caipirinhas. The drive from Buenos Aires to Jujuy was seventeen hours. Not desperate to do it without a stopover, they had interrupted their journey and booked into a hotel around four in the afternoon. Across the road from the bar was the buffet restaurant where they'd had a late lunch. The place had everything in the way of meat: *bife de chorizo, bife de lomo, vacío, tirada, chorizo, morcilla, chinchulines* – and it was the *chinchus,* the small intestines, which got Lucas. Beautiful medium-rare *bife de lomo* barbequed over oak wood was all he should have eaten. There was something about sitting opposite Gustavo, however, that made him eat a lot of everything fast. Maybe another plate of blood sausage and intestines and he'd feel less nervous? This had been his thought process. Now he was exceedingly full and concerned about being blocked up. Should he buy some laxatives?

A small girl appeared at their table with roughly carved wooden toucans and llamas for sale. Her clothes were dirty and she muttered her sales pitch without making eye contact. "Do you have any other animals?" Gustavo asked. She didn't understand. "A jaguar, for example," she seemed to get this and ran off.

Halfway through their second caipirinha, Gustavo unzipped his backpack and said, "Now I'm going to pass your share under the table." It occurred to Lucas that Gustavo was doing this now to catch him off guard. Handling significant amounts of cash on the street wasn't comfortable. The envelope felt light for the amount he was expecting. In the shop he'd handled many fake watches, and so was finely attuned to the weight of things. More commonly than its appearance, lack of weight betrayed a watch as a fake. He opened the envelope and counted out ten hundreds.

"Where's the rest? Our cut on the supermarkets was ten thousand. You gave me one thousand after the first one paid. So give me the three thousand more that I'm owed."

"I had to pay for the HiAce."

"I don't believe it. You said Ping wants us out of the country and I'm sure she provided the van. If not, then you stole it yourself." You never knew, maybe he had bought the vehicle, but Lucas had decided to put pressure on his partner. "I want the rest of my money."

Gustavo's arm moved like a striking snake and grabbed Lucas by the wrist. Lucas wasn't shocked. He'd expected this eventually. Gustavo's nails bored into his skin.

"Listen, I can take that thousand back if you want. You'd have no money at all without me."

Without Gustavo it was more likely he'd be rotting in the shop, figuring out how to pay next month's rent. That was preferable to being in this town halfway to the border, with the possibility the police were looking for them. Gustavo let go of his wrist and sat back in a relaxed posture, but the veins popping out of either side of his forehead gave him away. He would have been a handsome man if it wasn't for that angry, vascular, wrinkled forehead. Gustavo's street smarts and sinewy forearms let you know he was no novice in physical violence. Lucas outweighed him by ten kilos and was ten years younger, but he knew nothing about fighting. Unlike Gustavo, he hadn't had a tough upbringing. He guessed Gustavo had a knife in his pocket as well. At this stage, defusing the tension somewhat, the girl came back, bearing a couple of jaguars to choose from. Gustavo gave her three hundred pesos for one of them. Having only asked for one hundred, she ran off with a gap-toothed smile. There was no third caipirinha. They went off in different directions: Gustavo to the hotel and Lucas to the pharmacy.

Coming out of the pharmacy Lucas took a laxative and a drink of water. It would be better to let his stomach sit now. Should he go back to the hotel and rest? Not with Gustavo there. He got a beer from a store run by locals – no chinos in this part of the country yet. Then it didn't take long to find a quiet street where he could sit on the curb and relax, sipping the refreshing beer. Soon though, the peace was over. A car went by and two enraged street dogs emerged from somewhere to give chase. Finally, when the car turned the corner, they stopped barking. How many times had they pursued a car like this and almost gone under the wheels? They didn't chase for fun, it was a serious business, the car was on THEIR street. They wanted to cut the car off and bite the tyres, and so risked being run over. Lucas felt a flicker of admiration for these dogs. Their lives could end in starvation or sickness. Instead, they chose death fighting a mortal enemy, the invader of their kingdom. They'd made it until now, but if Lucas ever came back to this street, beauty and the beast would probably be gone. Beauty had a long muzzle and rich auburn fur. The beast was stocky with diseased skin.

A couple of teenagers in gothic get-ups came walking down the street eating empanadas. Both dressed all in black, one had a mime artist's white makeup job, the other a fringe down to the mouth. They sat down two metres away from Lucas, who now found himself looking a third street dog in the eye. An old animal, obviously sick and ready to drop, she had been handsome once. She looked like a purebred Labrador. Much skinnier than most pet Labradors, the imploring look in her eyes gave Lucas the idea she wasn't asking for food, but attention. Before he could decide whether to risk patting her, the dog left him for the androgynous teenagers. They lavished her with attention. Under their caresses, the old dog put on a sad show. She began swaying gently from side to side and then her head would drop. When she seemed about to fall over, she suddenly roused herself and straightened her neck with pride as the youths cheered her on. This cycle repeated itself countless times. This dog's car chasing days were behind her.

Lucas walked on, looking for another shop to buy beer in. He came to a plaza that was full of life. A homeless preacher with a matted beard and wild eyes captivated the attention of a small crowd. Quite an achievement, such characters were usually ignored. Lucas watched the man jump as if in a mosh pit and then do the eighties running man dance. These enthusiastic movements were intended to add weight to his nonsensical words: sentences from the Old Testament cut up and put back together randomly. As he danced, a rancid smell wafted through the air, but still the people stood in front of him. Energy and enthusiasm often counted more than content when you wanted to be listened to. Finally, the dancing preacher managed to utter something that made sense: "Then David said to himself, 'Now I will perish one day by the hand of Saul. There is nothing better for me than to escape into the land of the Philistines. Saul then will despair of searching for me anymore in all the territory of Israel, and I will escape from his hand.'" When compared with the other nonsense this seemed particularly meaningful, and Lucas walked off deep in thought, the plan to drink another beer and his *chinchulines*-induced digestive problems forgotten for the time being.

22

NECOCHEA

Gustavo had draped three clean shirts over the last row of seats in the HiAce van. *How did he do it?* Lucas wondered, giving the underarms of his t-shirt a smell. They were whiffy – he hadn't got his laundry done before leaving Buenos Aires. There wouldn't be an opportunity to wash clothes or get new ones for a while. Tomorrow or the day after, they would follow his plan to get across the border. An over-cautious plan according to Gustavo: "We can cross the border ourselves. The border guards won't stop us and if they do, there'll be no flags on the computer anyway." But Lucas's plan didn't involve much hassle, so Gustavo had agreed to it in the end.

They had been driving in silence for hours, but now Gustavo tried to strike up a conversation. "We could set up a restaurant in Bolivia, what do you think, Lucas? I hear there isn't much competition from the local places. Brazil is another option. I would like to be by the beach. We may get the go- ahead from Ping to return to Buenos Aires soon, I doubt it though..."

Lucas didn't respond to these plans of a future together. He was tired after his driving shift. Intrusive thoughts prevented him from getting to sleep. As a kid, when he couldn't sleep he thought about football, replaying in his head highlights of classic matches such as the 1994 World Cup game against Greece. The passion on Maradona's face after he scored a goal in that game was amazing. Lucas would remember the names and numbers of the Argentinian starting eleven and the replacements on the bench. Another distraction was listing the greatest goal scorers in *Primera División* history. He tried to remember these names and numbers now...but just as he was drifting off, Gustavo started talking again: "Necochea, do you know it? I guess the beaches in Brazil are better, but I liked Necochea and wanted to move there. My plan is on hold. Bloody Ping...first the Venezuelans now the Chinese making problems for us in our own country..."

Lucas wondered if Gustavo was trying to make a joke, nothing in his voice suggested it, however... He realised he'd better reply. "Yeah, I know Necochea. Nice, more tranquil than Mar del Plata."

"Better prices too," Gustavo said almost with a smile.

Lucas had been to Necochea on a family holiday as a child. His mother wanted to stay on the beach all day and be admired in her bikini. His dad found sunbathing dead boring and took Lucas on a long walk over to the nearby port of Quequén. The main attraction there was the Malvinas War Memorial, a giant monument made of four hundred and seventy tonnes of concrete and nearly forty metres high. Out of the circular base rose a triple-folded spire resembling a flame or, from some angles, a submarine tower. In the first fold sat a woman representing *La Patria*, a goddess of liberty type figure. On her lap lay a fallen soldier. Below *La Patria* were outlines of the Malvinas Islands and two large anchors.

"Do you know why the military government invaded the Malvinas, Lucas?" Even as a small boy Lucas knew his dad was asking a rhetorical question and he was in for a lecture. "The enemy without, Lucas... The military dictatorship was ruining the country. People hated the generals and admirals who had put themselves in charge. However, if they could win a war against a foreign enemy, it would spark patriotic emotion and make them popular. It didn't work, we lost the war, got smashed by the bloody British. The defeat was the death knell for the military government, paving the way for the return to democracy. I waved a flag in Plaza de Mayo when President Alfonsín made his speech about freedom. How naive! Look at how democracy has turned out, son. We might as well have the dictatorship back. At least they sorted out the criminals."

His father took no holidays from lecturing – what had he wanted his son to take out of his rants? That the system couldn't be trusted, that anything you tried would turn out badly, and the logical choice was to become an outlaw. No, this last one the old man would have never wanted for Lucas. However, his endless talks on the history of a broken nation planted that seed. Lucas wondered what Gustavo's Necochea had been like? Did he steal bags from holidaymakers on the beach, then bury them under the sand to pick them up later? Or just drink beers and chase girls? Maybe he spent the time in the sun dreaming of a better life. *No!* He had been stealing or something similar. He must not think of Gustavo sympathetically at this stage, it would be a big mistake.

23

THE ROCK

"You might call the border porous. It's not under the control of either the government of Argentina or Bolivia. Heading into Bolivia, you're going in the right direction because right now the gendarmerie officers are all nervously facing north. A couple of weeks ago they traded shots with some *contrabandistas* and ended up killing a child. We aren't sure how it happened. After, about five hundred people from the child's hometown in Bolivia crossed over and attacked the northernmost gendarmerie post in Argentina. They were repelled, but the rumour is they are looking to kill two gendarmerie men as revenge. We know some people from that town. They work as *bagayeros* for us when we need them. They're a tough lot."

"*Bagayeros*, what are they?" Lucas asked.

"You don't know much in Buenos Aires, do you? *Bagayeros* come over the border early in the morning and wait by the side of the road around two hundred metres north of any vehicle control stops the gendarmerie set up. When we come down the road with contraband on the roof of our car, we stop and the *bagayeros* help us unload. They walk away from the road with our stuff on their backs. We meet them again on the other side of the control stop. It's a farce the way it happens." Carlos was speaking, and he stopped now to spit out a wad of coca leaves. Carlos was the younger brother of Roberto. They were groove-faced men who had driven Lucas over the border for his first escape from Argentina into Bolivia.

Gustavo, not interested in border-region gossip, wanted to get to business, "How are we getting across? Why do we need you guys? It sounds like hundreds of people cross the border each day without worrying about customs or immigration control."

Carlos took a plastic bag of coca leaves out of his pocket and began stuffing them into his mouth. He didn't address any of Gustavo's questions. The Bolivian brothers wore lumberjack shirts of different colours from last time Lucas had seen them, or perhaps the colours were the same as before? Lucas couldn't remember. One difference for sure was they smiled. Being paid three hundred dollars had that effect, but Lucas reckoned they were also happy to see again the tall kid with greasy hair they had taken over the border a few months earlier. They slapped Lucas on the back and gave him mate and coca leaves. They offered these to Gustavo too, with less enthusiasm. The brothers had taken an instant dislike to him. The four of them sat around a plastic table in the shoe store in the Jujuy market.

"We'll go across in the station wagon with you, Roberto," Lucas said. "And Carlos can come across after in the white van."

"Two people in our car they haven't seen before might interest the border authorities. One of you should ride in the boot." Roberto said.

Gustavo smirked, "That's going to be you, Lucas."

"No, you will Gustavo. I say who rides where in my car," Roberto retorted, his face darkening.

Lucas looked at Gustavo. He saw the anger in his eyes and hoped the man would snap. If he turned violent against the brothers it might go badly for him, and Lucas would have his chance to get away. But Gustavo, his face a mask of control, backed down: "Very well, I'll go in the boot." Lucas's heart sank.

"And does the van have papers?" Roberto asked, "In case Carlos has to do an official crossing – get his passport stamped, etcetera." "Yes, it does," Gustavo answered.

"Let's have a look at them."

Grumbling, Gustavo got up and went out to where he'd parked the van. With him gone, Lucas racked his brain for something to say to the brothers to enlist their help against his tormentor. Nothing came to him. The three of them remained in amicable silence, passing the mate gourd around. Gustavo returned and the opportunity was lost. "Here they are," he handed the papers to Roberto, who took a look and handed them back.

"OK, we'll rendezvous on the other side at *estación central* in Villazón. There is only one café there. You can park out front."

***

Lucas knew the landscape on either side of the road would be desolate for a long stretch now. There was hardly any traffic: a vehicle coming the other way passed them every five minutes or so. "Drink some more water, you don't realise how dehydrated you're getting in this dry air. Your body loses water twice as fast as in Buenos Aires here. Once you are dehydrated the altitude will hit you."

"Alright, alright." Gustavo took his advice and chugged water from one of the two-litre bottles Lucas had bought in Villazón. An hour later Lucas was getting nervy, his companion seemed to have an iron bladder. Finally, two hours after saying goodbye to the brothers, and just after they passed some salt deposits, Gustavo told him to pull over. "Don't turn the engine off. I'm taking a quick piss."

Gustavo got out of the HiAce, stretched his back, and walked across the dusty ground. He stopped about ten metres from the van and was still visible from the road, but there would be no better chance. In the strong cold wind, Lucas flexed his fingers to prevent them from becoming numb. He opened the sliding door and on the back seat the rock was hidden under a blanket. He had agonised if it was the right size and weight to do the job, now it felt pleasantly heavy in his hands. He'd come prepared to avoid the nightmare of a perfect opportunity lost because of a patch of ground bereft of decent-sized loose rocks. He breathed in deeply, picked up the rock, and repeated the mantra as he crept up behind his prey: "Surprise beats experience, surprise beats experience." He waited until Gustavo had finished his piss; that seemed only fair. Then he didn't hesitate – do that and you are lost. The rock made a dull thud on impact. Gustavo fell down and then got up quickly. He made a slow, unsteady lunge at Lucas. The second blow did more damage and Gustavo landed on his bum. He was stunned. A thin red line trickled down the crevices of his forehead. Instead of the rage he expected, Lucas detected something else in Gustavo's eyes, perhaps an iota of respect. Surprise was there too. He'd had no inkling this was going to happen. Because of that look, Lucas could have let him live, but he needed to go through with it. On the fifth blow, there was a horrible cracking noise. Lucas felt disappointed at the amount of blood – he'd wanted it to pour out. The yellowy-brown ground the blood dribbled onto also let him down. He'd imagined light red rocks accepting the crimson liquid.

Searching his former tormentor's pockets, he found a folding hunter's knife and a wallet containing three hundred dollars and two thousand Argentine pesos. Gustavo should have spent the pesos already. No one would be offering a fair rate for them in Bolivia. The rest of Gustavo's cash and belongings were in his backpack, safely in the HiAce. The cops, or whoever found him, would get the gold-plated Diesel Big Daddy watch and the pesos as reward. What if nobody came?

Lucas stood in the cold wind, running his hands through his hair. He imagined Gustavo's skin beginning to change colour and blister, the abdomen bulging, then the first rupture and an explosion of fluid from the nose. At some stage the vultures – or did they have condors here? –

would come and eat Gustavo's *chinchulines*. There would be maggots, a smell of putrefaction, and eventually only bones covered by scraps of clothing. Leaving the man's corpse to this fate struck him as terrible, but why? No, nonsense, the smell of money would bring men long before the corpse began to break down. Lucas took the hundreds from Gustavo's wallet and three hundred from his own. The morgue worker would find six hundred dollars in the dead man's shoes.

***

Thank you for taking the time to read *Buenos Aires Triad*. Please consider leaving a rating or review on Amazon and/or Goodreads.

NOTE

Note on currency: I've tried to keep the numbers here simple. However, to retain some realism, I needed to include both Argentine pesos and American dollars. The peso has been losing ground against the dollar since 2001. As a couple of points of reference: in 2004, three pesos were equal to one American dollar, and in April 2021, it was ninety pesos to the dollar. I have used a rate of sixty pesos to one dollar as the official government rate, and seventy-two to one as the black market or *dólar blue* rate. Prices for large items in Argentina are often quoted in dollars, as the price in pesos changes so quickly. If one can get them, dollars are used for savings as they hold their value. Several governments have placed exchange restrictions, so pesos cannot be freely exchanged for dollars. The aims of these are to prevent capital flight, further devaluation of the peso, and inflation. The peso is very much the currency of day-to-day transactions.